Ink & Brazen Women

I0745722

Skin deep

CASSIE LEIGH

Copyright © 2017 Cassie Leigh
All Rights Reserved

Cover design © Cover Couture
http://www.bookcovercouture.com
Photos © Depositphotos
Formatting by AB Formatting

All characters, events, and locations are fictitious. Any resemblance to persons, past, present, or future is coincidental and highly unlikely.

Sassy Typewriter Press
5001 1st Ave SE
Ste. 105 #243
Cedar Rapids, IA 52402
https://sassy.typewriter.press/

ISBN 978-1-940509-27-3

Version 1.0.1

This book is dedicated to my husband, Ryan. On publication date, we will have just celebrated our 11ᵗʰ wedding anniversary and 14 years together. We met on the internet when dial up was still a thing and our life has taken us in some crazy places. I was young and you trusted me with your daughters and your heart. You allow me to grow and change in directions you didn't know you signed up for and we still choose each other even when things are difficult. Thank you.

acknowledgements

I owe a lot to my editor Barbara, as well as my publisher Dylan Moonfire for creating Sassy Typewriter Press and helping me through this publishing experience. Every new project is an adventure and we learn a little more. I also would like to say thank you to the Noble Pen writing group. They read the early chapters of this book and their advice helped it to take shape. During the final growing pains of this novel, there were also very loyal Beta readers who cheered me on. Krystal, Jennifer, Patricia, and Peggy—you all helped push this one through to the end. And a special thanks to Allison, Heidi and Charlotte for coming through in the clinch when the Copy Edit panic hit. I swear I lost epic amounts of sleep I will never get back. Thank you for putting up with my crazy.

This book tested my limits and my endurance. It frustrated me but it also kept me in its grips. It demanded that I make it a series instead of a standalone and it defied my obsessive need to plot ahead. All of this because I saw an image of a woman and I knew her story—that's how Ink & Brazen Women was born. Anna Crosswell, your cover inspired this journey and laid the foundation for a series. Your work amazes me.

You should know this novel is different than anyone knew I was capable of writing. Brace yourself because it's bolder and not the sweet romance you might expect based on my early books. I counted curse words while I edited. This is not clean. Gigi Duval has fire and vulnerability that I found I could identify with, but still takes chances. This also taught me things about myself. While I wrote this, I physically changed and took my own risks that I never would have before. That's a tall order for one book. I hope you love or at least appreciate Skin Deep as much as I do!

chapter 1

*t*here were few things more uncomfortable than the morning after—awkward text messages, ignored phone calls, or the not so random meeting in the street. As Gigi Duval deleted yet another dick pic off her phone, she decided last night's fuckboy was testing every one.

She took another sip of her latte and then forced a sociable smile on her perfectly glossed lips. She'd met her best friend, Ann Kennedy, for coffee at their favorite café in the rehabbed NewBo neighborhood. She loved the brick building with its original tin ceiling, high gloss wood tables and metal bistro chairs. It smelled like freshly brewed coffee and soul.

"Which play date is harassing you now?" Ann

asked with a knowing smirk, one expertly drawn blonde eyebrow raised.

They were meeting over Ann's lunch break, so she dressed accordingly in a navy silk top and khaki cropped dress slacks. Her severe, flat-ironed hair and neutral makeup choices were selected with a strategic eye to reflect her poised businesswoman image.

Gigi turned the phone face down as it dinged yet again. She tapped her pink polished nails on the floral plastic case in annoyance. "One whose name will be erased from my little pink book when I get home."

"Sounds like you didn't enjoy your walk of shame."

Some variation of this conversation started most of Gigi's lunch dates with her best friend. You would think Gigi called a new date every night. Her lips curved up into a smile as her shoulders raised in a non-committal shrug. "Don't be ridiculous—I prefer the term slut strut."

"I can't wait for someone to catch your eye for more than a quick fling," Ann sighed as she pushed a piece of salad across her plate. "You can't keep this up forever. It's not safe."

Gigi shrugged, brushing off her concern. Men caught her eye on a regular basis. The problem was choosing one. Years ago, she learned men could have as many women as they wanted and no one seemed to care. So why couldn't she have the same? Who made the rule that she couldn't have no-strings-sex and save her heart from one brutal let down after another?

Did she ever get tired of it? Absolutely. She was tempted to retire the little pink book all the time. Just last night for example. She sat waiting for Dick Pic—a colossal waste of time—when a tattooed god-among-men had approached her and offered to buy her a drink. *You're too classy for a dive like this, beautiful.* He hadn't been rude or handsy. He just sat there chatting with her, keeping her company and the lechers away until her date arrived—a full thirty minutes late—and then drifted back to his friends.

"What are you up to today besides mischief?" Ann asked.

Gigi released the breath she had been holding at Ann's sudden change in topic. "Just chasing job leads and then dinner with the parents. Nothing too exciting."

"Speaking of family connections, would you like a new lead?" Ann reached into her Kate Spade bag and pulled out her tablet, an iPad Pro that Gigi had been salivating over for months. "My step-brother just opened a tattoo shop and needs someone to be his office manager. Just basic stuff, run the front desk, setup and run his website. Nothing you haven't done before."

Grabbing a business card out of the tablet's case, she slid it across the table. Gigi picked it up, running her fingertips over the embossed skull design.

A tattoo shop wasn't exactly the kind of place she would have applied. She also hadn't planned on leaving the bank, but her former employer cornered her in his office for a little quid pro quo. She gave her immediate notice to the HR department. The ink wasn't even dry on her resignation before she was out the door. Now it had been a month and her savings would only hold out so much longer. At the very least, this could tide her over while she found something else.

"I'll pop down there and give him my resume." Gigi slipped the card into her purse and picked up her latte for another sip. "But I'm keeping my options open."

Ann rolled her eyes as she put her tablet away. "Just do me a favor and keep his name out of your book?"

Sighing, Gigi placed her hand over her heart as if wounded. "For shame. That would be breaking rule number three and potentially number six. No screwing those with a connection to your life and no fucking around in the workplace. I left a job over that. I'm not exactly looking to repeat the experience."

Ann was one of the few people who knew about

the rules. They'd become fast friends when they met at a mixer for young professionals and discovered they'd been unknowingly sharing the same male companion. Gigi may not engage in relationships but she did abide by strict rules—the first being: all parties must be single. No cheaters were welcome in her bed. Ann was delighted to dodge a bullet and the two women had been friends ever since.

Friendship and trust were two commodities that Gigi didn't deal in often. In life, all you had was your reputation and Gigi guarded hers closely. That's why she had created the rules and cultivated the perfect disguise. She masqueraded as the kind of girl that one would take home to mother, in a package of petite pink innocence, right down to her toe nail polish. The boys liked this virtuous façade too, because despite her rules, she had no trouble filling the space on her proverbial dance card when she wanted it.

"I have your promise then?" Ann's tone had dropped to a level of seriousness normally directed at her employees—not her friends—and with her brow furrowed and lips pressed together, her expression formed a stern mask.

That question—the doubt it implied—made Gigi's eyes burn as the latte soured in her stomach. She looked away. This was the downside of her choices. Logically, Gigi knew that Ann wasn't intentionally slut shaming her. Her friend was protecting someone she cared for. It still made Gigi's skin crawl as though she were nothing more than a cheap whore. She'd promise almost anything to make that feeling go away.

"I promise." Those two small whispered words should have been the easiest she uttered all day. Instead, they etched her throat like acid.

chapter 2

the Red Barron wasn't the kind of place Roman Bishop ever would have expected to see an angel. This place was a dive in the truest sense of the word, with hard music, cheap beer, and dark corners. Damn—he wanted to see her light up one of those corners.

Swathed in a soft pink dress and white fuck-me heels, she had him entranced. She moved the curtain of her dark hair, exposing the graceful curve of her shoulder, a creamy canvas that made his hand tingle with the phantom buzz of his tattoo gun. It would be a fucking honor to mark her. The glow of that lovely skin had drawn him away from his friends like a moth to her flame. Hell—he had never seen a woman *like her and he was no virgin schoolboy fumbling in the dark.*

"You're too classy for a dive like this, beautiful." He slid into the vacant seat beside her even as he cringed inwardly at his own cheesy pickup line. "Are you lost?"

She turned clear absinthe green eyes his direction and his breath caught.

Her full lips teased a soft smile. "Just waiting for my date. He's late."

Roman's heart sank. Of course, a girl that gorgeous wouldn't be alone. "Can I at least keep you company? I'll buy you a drink and keep the riffraff in this joint at bay."

Great, now he sounded like a desperate ass. If she minded, she didn't show it. If anything, her smile grew and she turned more fully his direction.

"I've got a drink." She held up her wine glass as evidence—yet another sign she was too much for this shithole. "But I would welcome the company."

They chatted for ten minutes. Every word confirmed her as both witty and intelligent, proving she was more than just perfumed eye candy. He almost wished that's all she would have been. If her mind had been inferior to the package on the outside, he could have enjoyed the view and forgotten her, but now... He cut the thought off as the shadow of her date loomed over them—literally.

"Am I interrupting something?" Her date looked like a yuppie, complete with chinos and a striped polo. Why the hell would a guy like that have her wait here?

She glanced at the dainty gold watch on her wrist. "Waiting for you. You're thirty minutes late."

Yuppie-boy held out his hand for her with a cocky smirk that Roman's fingers itched to bitch-slap off his face. "Don't worry, doll. I'll make it up to you."

"We'll see about that." Her smile turned sugar sweet as she slid out of the barstool. She did not take his hand, instead brushing past him towards the exit. "Are you coming?"

Leaning towards Roman, while eyeing her admittedly fine ass, her date whispered as if they'd been frat brothers or some shit. "She's sassy and demanding but totally worth the ride."

The sleazebag—he'd been downgraded— hurried to catch up to her and hold the door. She looked back at Roman and her smile warmed. It hadn't met her eyes when she smiled at her date. She'd given that gift to Roman, and he didn't even know her name.

Roman's pencil tip dug into the front desk. His mind forced back from the memory he'd been drifting in as Declan Stone, his best friend and fellow artist, yanked the sketchpad away. Roman made an ineffectual grab for the spiral bound paper.

"What the hell, man?"

Declan leaned back in his chair, holding the artwork just out of reach. "Just checking out what you're doin'." He tossed the book down in front of Roman and pointed at the pinup girl meticulously drawn from memory on the page. "You've been spaced out since that chick last night."

"Yeah, so what?"

"So forget about it. She left with somebody else."

His friend was right. She did leave, but something about that look on her face as she had—as if she resigned herself to it but really wasn't interested. A woman like her could have anyone, which left him wondering why she'd gone, instead of telling the douche canoe to fuck off. Ultimately, it wasn't his place to get involved. In the rare down time he had between clients, he had better things to do than moon over the one who got away—like keeping the doors to their shop open.

Ink Spinners Tattoo & Gallery had been a dream and a labor of love for both Roman and Declan—one whose timetable moved up thanks to Roman's ex. The old brick building was one of the last the NewBo District had saved. They closed on the purchase just one week before the wrecking ball and saved it from becoming a new urban development made to look vintage. Thanks to the local historical society, they got it for a song and spent the better part of the year renovating it. Now the shop looked as if a steampunk barbershop and a Victorian apothecary had a baby. For a couple of black sheep local boys, they were doing all right.

Roman dragged his hand over the rough stubble of his jaw. "You're right. Not like I could find her if I wanted to."

"Funny you should say that." A cocky grin split Declan's face just as the bell over the door rang.

Roman turned, smile at the ready as the girl in question sauntered through the door. "Damn."

Her steps faltered at his whispered oath, but he couldn't help himself. Ten seconds ago, he had no hope of ever seeing her again, let alone in his shop. Good girls like her don't have ink. Everything about her whispered that he was right, especially the way she dressed today; a blush pink blazer, layered over a white t-shirt that she tucked into a pink and black rose patterned pencil skirt. She had tamed the dark curls he remembered from last night into a bun, and oversized pearl earrings hung from earlobes that he already visualized sucking on.

"You're Ann's step-brother?" Her voice held the same breathless wonder that he uttered his own curse in seconds before. When she continued, her tone was brighter, with crisp efficiency. "I'm here about the job. Ann Kennedy referred me."

The attitude switch about gave him whiplash.

She held out her hand and as he stood to take it, her soft, slender fingers seemed swallowed up by his darker, tattooed mitt. "Roman Bishop and this is my business partner, Declan Stone, you are…"

"Oh yeah, I'm Gigi Duval." She stared up into his eyes, leaving her hand in his for longer than necessary before she seemed to notice and pull back.

He forced down a groan at the simple loss of her warmth in his hand. She wet her pouty pink lips. When his gaze zeroed in on the subtle movement, the corners turned up, ever so slightly. This couldn't be good. Mere moments into formally meeting her and he was already smitten. Would it be strange to propose marriage now? Oh wait—she had a boyfriend—at least she did last night.

Gigi would give anything to rollback her day to lunch and hand that card back to Ann or better yet, keep the card and refuse to give that forced promise. Life could be an unforgiving bitch and right now, life clearly had it in for Gigi. Why did it have to be him?

There was no one in the history of man that made

a plain white t-shirt and jeans look that good—except maybe James Dean. Roman's clothes weren't plain. They were a statement. A white wall, allowing the brilliant color and bold black lines of ink running up both arms to speak for him. Her panties were insta-soaked just imagining tracing each intricate design with her tongue. Add to that, the amber fire of his eyes, he was just too much. Roman Bishop was the worst kind of temptation.

If she hoped to keep that ill-fated vow, let alone her precious rules, she would need to turn tail and run back the way she came. Unfortunately, her fat mouth must be under the sway of her hormones or her dwindling bank account.

"Ann said you need an office manager. So here I am, resume in hand." She whipped out a crisp sheet of paper from her folder as evidence. He took it without even glancing at the words. "Has the position been filled?"

"You're hired." His voice held a note of awe and his eyes seemed to spark.

"I'm sorry? Aren't you going to interview me?" She raised one eyebrow as she looked from Roman to Declan, who stood chuckling beside him.

He leaned forward across the desk, his fingers gripping the edge, turning his knuckles white. "If you couldn't do the job, Ann wouldn't have sent you. You need a job. I have one to fill. What more do I need to know?"

"I have a few questions if you don't." Gigi took a step back towards the door as she said it.

This was not how this should have gone, despite his assurance that it only reflected trust in his sister. Something about the way he looked at her like a hopeful lost puppy—the way he had last night—made her worry this might not end well for her. He seemed like a nice enough guy in the bar, but she didn't want an attachment and, of course, there was that damned promise to consider. She had to keep reminding herself.

Roman ran his hand through his slicked back hair with a bashful half-cocked smile. "Yeah, I suppose you do. I guess I should have thought of that."

"For starters, what would be my responsibilities—hours, salary? You know—the basics." Then at least she could tell Ann it wasn't a good fit, rather than admit she couldn't be around her friend's delectable step-brother.

"We're open Tuesday through Saturday and you would work the front desk, taking appointments, answering phones, that kind of thing." Roman looked back at his friend, as if expecting him to chime in. The big guy nodded and Roman continued. "But you'll have help with that because your primary job will be the website and the gallery. We do an art show every other month. You would be in charge of that. Would you like to see it—the gallery, I mean?"

"Absolutely."

He walked around the edge of the counter and extended his hand out to direct her towards a black partition wall erected on the left side of the space. A three-dimensional skull of layered gears decorated the wall. He followed behind her as she moved to the gallery entrance. He never touched her, but the awareness of his hand hovering at the small of her back had a physical force as they walked. She dismissed it as wishful thinking—her inner sadist wanting someone she shouldn't have.

She hugged her leather folder to her chest as if it would somehow shield her from her own desire as she wandered through the maze of black walls. The paintings ranged from dark and exotic to colorful pop art using mixed media.

"Are they all yours?" She asked, her voice embarrassingly breathless.

He paused in front of a gothic looking piece of a broken man on his knees, screaming in agony.

"Mine are in here," he said, gesturing up at the painting in question. "Most are from the other artists who work here. I'd like to feature artists who come through to do a guest spot in the shop."

His thoughtful expression as he examined it made her wonder if he'd painted this one to represent himself. She had a strong urge to soothe whatever caused that level of pain. There were so many shadowy corners back here for her to do just that.

It could be so easy to back him into one of those dark spaces right now. If it weren't for that promise or rule number three, she would get down on her knees and find a different job later. It would almost be worth it to see the rest of his ink.

She shook herself from her dirty thoughts with a shaky indrawn breath and took a step back, as if physical distance would lessen his pull on her. "Have you thought about renting the space for parties? I could imagine a great upscale office event here."

A smile split his previously pensive face. "See that's why you're perfect for this job. I need that kind of outside-the-box thinking." He jammed his hands in his front pockets and kicked at some unseen spot on the floor. "I know color and how to make beautiful art. How to use it in business... I'm not a businessman. I mean I own one but..."

"I get it. You need marketing help. I know how to do that."

His shoulders sagged in apparent relief at her understanding. "I probably can't pay you what you're used to or even what you deserve, not at first. If you're okay with that, the job is yours."

"This wasn't exactly what I was expecting." His expression dropped like a disappointed toddler and she rushed to amend her statement. "It's better than I expected. That being said, I'd like to think on it and get back to you."

His return smile was hesitant, which didn't render it any less heart stopping. "I can respect that. Just let me know if you have any more questions."

They continued through the maze of walls in silence until they were back where they started.

"I'll be at the Red Barron again tonight if you feel the need to talk it through or have any more questions." His voice was quiet and deep, just for her, as he closed the distance between them. If that wasn't a blatant reminder of his attraction to her the night before, she'd burn her little pink book—or maybe not. "If you're worried about what your boyfriend will think, I won't make it weird."

"He wasn't my boyfriend." The words slipped out without thought, but she didn't regret them. Not when another smile lit up his face. Despite the false hope of his openness, she found it intoxicating. She should be ashamed of herself for encouraging it, but it made her want to swoon just the same.

"Thanks for the tour." Gigi held her hand out to him, waiting anxiously for him to take it.

Roman took it, trapping her small hand between both of his. A thrill ran through her and she choked back the sharp indrawn breath threatening to break free, carefully schooling her features into passive awareness with a tight smile. *Rules, Gigi. Remember the rules.* Was she aware that she was pathetic for being excited over this small shred of physical contact with him? Yes. Clearly, she was going to have to call in a date to fuck the edge off, because there was no way she could ever hook up with Roman Bishop.

chapter 3

utiful daughter—yet another role Gigi play-acted her way through on a semi-regular basis. With another rule—*thou shalt keep up appearances*. Thanks to her wasted afternoon of job hunting, she was in no mood for it. She pasted that smile on anyway just in case someone was looking as her kitten heels tapped out each step up the flagstone walkway.

Her attendance and feigned positive attitude were the least she could do for her long-suffering mother. Besides, she missed the two-story brick house of her youth, even if she didn't miss the people in it. They led an ideal life here, picture perfect on the outside. Her father, John Duval, and his successful law firm provided enough for her mother to stay home and live the life of a suburban carpool mom. They'd even had the perfect number of children in the perfect order. Her older brother, John Junior, had been smart enough to ride an athletic scholarship right out of town. Gigi hadn't been so lucky, hence her obligatory weekly dinner with the parents.

She crossed her mother's pristine threshold, softly closing the door painted a high gloss black lacquer. Classic was always best. Leslie Duval lived those words as if they were a coat of arms.

"Gigi, darling, is that you?" Her mother poked her head out of the kitchen door, not one glossy curl out of place. They looked more like sisters than mother and daughter.

"Are you expecting someone else?"

"Your father invited a friend from the firm." From the downturn of her lips and brow creases that defied regular Botox injections, Leslie was not pleased about it.

"Great." Gigi forced her thin smile to hold with just the right false note of cheer.

This evening's regular activity of polite conversation would now be compounded by her father's attempt to arrange her life in a way he deemed respectable enough. Wouldn't he just shit if he knew where she'd been offered a job? That brought the first true smile to her face that she'd probably worn all afternoon.

"Will you be a dear and set the table? I've already pressed the tablecloth and spread it over the table. Your father hates if it's not perfect and you always do such a lovely job." Her mother made a valiant effort to force a smile but it came across openly anxious. Leslie wore her emotions like a transparent billboard. It remained a frequent source of criticism from Gigi's father.

Contrary child that Gigi was, she adored this small fault in her mother and couldn't say no when her mother looked at her so openly. "I'd be happy to, Mom." A statement that couldn't be further from the truth.

Leslie ducked back into her kitchen, leaving Gigi to carry out her assigned task. She hung her bag on a hook in the closet and walked down the hall decorated straight out of *Midwest Living* magazine, the rug silencing the echo from her footsteps. Gigi paused at the entryway into the dining room.

The door to her father's office stood ajar, allowing the deep murmur of his voice to carry across the hall. He often conducted business from home. Gigi stepped lightly across the distance to pull the door closed and give him some privacy, but her hand froze on the door handle.

"Baby, you know I can't see you tonight. I have company. Tomorrow. I'll tell her I have to work late and I'll come over. Or you can stop in my office and let me have you for lunch." The teasing note in his voice made Gigi's stomach turn.

She wished she could say it was the first time. The man was careless enough that Gigi had caught him a handful of times through the years. If it was that easy for her, she could only imagine what her mother had discovered him doing. Gigi had even tried to tell her mother the first couple of times but it was clear that she didn't want to hear. It seemed she thrived on denial.

Gigi drew in a slow steady breathe as she pulled the door closed with a soft click and crossed the hall to her mother's china cabinet. She counted the seconds on each breath as she took down the plates and glasses. Twenty.

The door across the hall cracked open and her father's balding head poked out. "Oh, Gigi, it's you. How long have you been here?"

She visualized smashing the fine white china from her parents' wedding over his head one plate at a time. Instead, she stretched her lips into a thin smile. "Not long. Mom asked me to set the table; she said you'd be having a guest join us for dinner." She moved over to the table clutching the china.

Gigi carefully set out each plate. Keeping her eyes averted from her father as he crossed the hall to her. He circled like a shark looking for weakness. This was not an unusual occurrence for John, especially when company was anticipated. He required everything he owned to be perfect; his daughter was no exception.

"I'm glad to see you dressed up today." It was the closest thing to approval she was likely to get from him.

"I had interviews." Gigi offered as she retrieved the linen napkins and silverware from the drawer where her mother kept them stored for special occasions. If she kept moving, maybe he'd drop the conversation and go back to calling his floosy.

"Your mother told me about the unfortunate event." Of course, her mother had, but her father wasn't finished. "Have you considered suing? I can't take your case naturally. I have colleagues who would be happy too."

"No, Dad." She continued to move around the table while he stood stoically observing her from the doorway. "I'd like to just find a new position and continue on with my life."

Truth was, she had considered it. As the daughter of a lawyer, complete with summer internships, she was keenly aware of how invasive the process could be into one's personal life, especially for the woman. That alone was enough to rule out a lawsuit. One look into her life and dating habits would kill any chance she had. Liking consensual sex and not wanting a commitment were not crimes and if she had been a man, it would have been fine. As a woman, the incident with her boss would be turned on its head.

The details painted as something she provoked and her employer the victim. It wasn't right but it happened.

"Perhaps you should move home."

If he had been a loving father and not someone bent on control she might have found the offer sweet, but John Duval had an angle for everything.

Gigi shook her head no, as she leaned across the table, adding a water glass and wine glass to each setting. "Thanks, Dad, but I have a good lead on an office manager position. I'm doing just fine."

He opened his mouth to argue, but the doorbell saved her. Leslie swept in from the kitchen, set down a pitcher of ice water and bustled out towards the front door like the hurricane homemaker that she was, John following behind her.

Leslie pulled the door open and stepped back into her place at John's side to allow their guest entrance. John's arm went around Leslie's waist like the picture of an adoring husband. It made Gigi want to gag. This was why she did what she did—the lying. At least she knew the score. No one would cheat on her like that if she didn't settle down. Even her own father, who cared so much for his image, couldn't be bothered to settle down. If Mister Perfect couldn't handle monogamy, what chance did another, imperfect man have?

Her attention shifted to their guest. Dick Pic was shaking her father's hand. Fan-fucking-tastic.

"So glad you could make it, Chad." John turned, clasping the young attorney's shoulder, guiding him to face Gigi. "You've already met my wife. This is my daughter, the one I told you about."

"I've actually met Gigi. We have mutual friends." An oily smile spread across his clean-cut, boy-next-door façade—evidently his professional front.

Yesterday, she found Chad's grin annoying, but not enough to keep from attempting what turned out to be a lackluster bedroom performance. As she scrolled through her phone at lunch, his actions had only irritated her. Now, revulsion coiled in her stomach. The fact that her father told Chad about her rendered last night and his barrage of sext messages today in a creepier light. The possibility that he planned to use their casual arrangement against her father made her shudder with disgust. She struggled to keep it from showing on her forced blank expression. The Tinder dating pool had suddenly become too shallow. Definitely should have swiped left.

"Oh, I almost forgot." Chad turned and presented a bottle of wine to Leslie. "I didn't know what we were having so I went with a white. I hope that's okay?"

"Chad, that's so sweet. I'll just go open this up. Gigi, will you come and help me bring dinner to the table?" The strained note in her voice showed she knew something was up. Her mother wouldn't help herself, but she was perceptive when it came to her offspring.

"Sure thing, Mom." Anything to escape from this awkward mess.

The fact that she couldn't spend thirty minutes with her parents without looking for an escape spoke volumes about her life. Now, having to spend her evening with both Chad and her parents—keeping up appearances—this was a new level of nightmare even for her standards. She needed out.

No sooner had the kitchen door swung closed then her mother turned on her, her voice a low hush. "Tell me what's wrong, Gigi."

Now here was the balancing act. Her parents had no idea how she behaved. To them she was still their virginal little girl, someone they needed to shelter and protect. They had no idea about the male friends on call for a quick hookup and until tonight, it had never crossed into their lives. She also refused to lie to her mother.

Gigi settled for a watered-down version of the truth as she leaned against the counter, arms crossed protectively in front of her. "I went on a date with him last night. It didn't go well and now I wonder if he asked me out just because of Dad. I didn't plan to see him again so this makes me really uncomfortable."

Leslie reached out, stroking Gigi's arm in

sympathy. "Then I guess we are just going to have to get you out of here."

"Dad will be so mad." She sighed, slumping forward.

She sounded like a petulant kid, not a twenty-five-year-old professional with her life in order. Dealing with her parents always seemed to bring that out in her. Mostly she managed to keep it together unless something threw her for a loop. Dick Pic was one major loop in her carefully stitched cover.

Leslie held out the now opened bottle of wine and a basket of rolls. "Get out there and then beg off to the bathroom. If you play sick, your Father will look bad if he's unsympathetic. He'll have to let you go."

Leave it to Mom to find a way around that wouldn't make waves. "Thank you for helping." Gigi wanted to tell her, use that same logic and get yourself out. If after thirty years of marriage she didn't see it, she probably never would.

Gigi took the offered items, then took a deep breath to gird herself for the performance she was about to give. She appeared fine moments before, so she would need to be subtle but obvious enough to get by. She allowed her shoulders to slump and her smile to slide away as she returned to the dining room. Setting the bread in the center of the table and the bottle in front of Chad, she took the open seat beside him. Leslie followed with the lasagna.

Gigi took a tentative sip from her water glass.

John broke the awkward silence as he dished his serving of pasta onto his plate. "Chad, how did the two of you meet? I know you said mutual friends but there must be more to it than that."

Her hand flew to her mouth as she struggled not to choke on the water. She forced it down and cut in just as Chad opened his mouth to answer. "Do you remember that group for young professionals I told you about? We met at one of their events. We know some people in common."

If her father's glare could have struck her with lightning, he likely would have. If she had been ten, she would have been backhanded for speaking out of turn when Chad had clearly been the one her father had been addressing. She'd deal with it later, because she knew better than to think she wouldn't get the riot act about her lapse in manners.

Chad smiled politely, poured a glass of wine for himself and then for Gigi before passing the bottle to her father. "I didn't get to spend enough time with her, but she made an impression."

Clammy fingers groped her knee under the tablecloth, sliding up her bare thigh—shades of last night's adolescent level attempt. Chad wasn't even looking at her as he did it. He was smiling at her father. Oh yeah, this come on to her was about fucking the boss's daughter—total sleazebag. She'd love nothing more than to stab a fork in his wandering hand right there.

As his fingertips grazed the edge of her panties, she jumped, pushing her chair back from the table. "Excuse me, I'll be right back."

Gigi rushed from the room with one hand over her mouth and the other straightening her skirt. The power trip Chad had to be feeling right now at her expense didn't make it difficult to act nauseated. She rushed up the stairs, into the bathroom. When she reached the sink, she carefully splashed cold water on her exposed skin.

Between displays like the one downstairs from the fuckboys she tended to attract, and the philandering of her father, she found an endless string of reminders why relationships were a waste of time. If her dates treated her like an object, it became easier to treat men the same.

There—she just needed this reminder. She could go work for Roman without any fear of temptation, especially if it meant avoiding moving back home and any further entanglement with her father's setups like Chad. Yep, as soon as she escaped, she was heading down to Red Barron to accept the job.

Leaning on her forearms against the granite counter with her head bent over the sink, Gigi heard the door behind her creak open. She looked up into the mirror past her own pallid face. Now she really did want to vomit.

"The guest bathroom is downstairs at the end of the hall, Chad." Gigi kept her voice hushed. God forbid it carry down to her parents.

He dry humped her ass. "That's not the kind of relief I was looking for."

She slid to the right and was almost out of his grasp, when Chad reached out and snatched her wrist. "I can't do this here. This is my parents' house. Did you know that last night?"

"I thought I'd surprise you."

She wanted to slap that grin off his face. She might still if he didn't let go of her. "It wasn't really a pleasant surprise."

"Don't be like that. I thought you like it a little dirty, princess." He pulled her against him, his breath hot on her neck as he ground his erection into her hip.

"I'm not playing with you." She jerked her wrist free and rushed from the room.

Gigi made it back downstairs without his answering footfalls chasing behind her. Thank fuck for small miracles. He was at least keeping up appearances, even if it was only because he worked for her father. She would take that reason if it helped her cause.

She stumbled into the dining room and leaned heavily on the chair. "Dad, I'm so sorry. I think whatever I had for lunch is making me sick. I'm going to have to go."

"Sit down." Her father's voice was sharp and commanding, his face pinched in frustration. "You were fine when you got here. I will not have you embarrassing me in front of my company. You will sit and make it through this dinner."

"John, let her go. She's a grown woman. You can't order her like a child." Her mother laid a restraining hand on his forearm. "Besides wouldn't it be worse for her to be sick at the table? She looks awfully pale."

Gigi gripped the back of the chair and concentrated on looking pathetic; hating that at twenty-five she still needed his permission. The longer she stood there, the sooner Chad would be joining them. Was her father's consent more important than being stuck fending off Chad's inappropriate advances? Easy answer—she'd rather face her father's ire.

"Please give Chad my apologies."

John's face burned red. She turned her back on him. As she rushed down the hall, she scooped her bag off the closet hook and was out the front door before her father could regain enough control to launch a tirade that she'd certainly receive later on.

There were bigger things to worry about. Just how committed to this was Chad? It was a damn good thing they'd been at his place and not hers last night. A shudder ran down her spine as she settled into her Fiat. Thanks to this debacle, that would be added to her rules—no one comes to her place until properly vetted.

chapter 4

Stop watching the damn door and start watching the fight." Declan waved toward the flat screen, his amused tone grating Roman's already frayed nerves.

They came to the Red Barron to watch one of Roman's regular clients, Ion Constantin, cage fight in the big leagues of MMA. Ion had brought in plenty of referrals from the gym after Roman finished his sleeve and they genuinely liked the kid. They'd been watching him kick ass in the local circuit for the last year. Now that Ion was getting his shot in the big time, they wouldn't miss the chance to see him tear up his opponent. Roman would just have to stop eyeing the door long enough to see it.

"I'll bet you anything that chick ain't coming back. A girl like that thinks she's too good to work at a tattoo shop." Declan traced the edge of his glass with his ring finger, the good humor gone and a dark look in his eyes.

There was a story behind that statement. Roman only knew a small piece. Declan had been carrying a torch for Roman's stepsister since they were just a couple of kids at the skate park. At one point Roman caught them kissing in the backyard, but she'd gone off to college and started dating yuppies who wore ties and Rolexes. Nothing but high class for Ann and heartbreak for Declan—not that the moody ass would admit it.

Roman leaned forward, slapping his hand on the table hard enough to slosh the beer in their tallboys. "I'll take that bet."

Declan hadn't seen the way Gigi lit up when they rounded the wall into the gallery space. Excitement burned in her eyes at what the gallery could be. Even though she'd left this bar with a guy that was more Ann's speed, if Roman had to guess, the douchebag wasn't the kind of guy that set Gigi on fire. He wasn't so sure she was the picture of innocent sophistication she was presenting. If she walked through that door, he planned to strip her bare and find out just what kind of girl she really hid under that veneer.

"Oh no—if she comes in here and takes the job

you are staying away from this one. I know that look in your eyes. Have you forgotten about Jessica already?"

"Gigi is not Jessica."

"How do you know? You only just met this girl."

"This girl already has class. Jessica was just looking for a sugar daddy." Roman relaxed in his chair, propping his boots up in the empty chair in front of him.

Declan pointed at Roman with one eyebrow raised. "That's not what you thought before she fucked around with Lou." Declan shook his head like he was clearing cobwebs. "Shit man, I'm sorry. That was a low blow."

Lou owned the shop he and Declan worked at before they went into business for themselves. Jessica had done piercings and operated the front desk. He should probably thank Jessica for sucking off their boss. Roman might have waited to leave the shop and would have missed his chance at the great spot in NewBo if he hadn't forgotten the engagement ring he'd planned to give her that night. He walked in on Lou standing in his office, ass hanging out and Jessica on her knees in front of him.

"Fuck them—and fuck you too. You taking the bet or not?"

"Why not—drinks are on the loser." Declan

shrugged. "If she comes, you're gonna need to get shitfaced when she breaks your heart and then drinks will be on you. I'll win either way."

Turned out they didn't have to wait long. Gigi came in like a pink storm cloud. The spark in her green eyes, crackled with the lightning of her mood. She wove through the sparse Friday evening crowd and he swore he could hear the echo of thunder in her wake. He wasn't sure if he should be thanking whoever pissed her off so that he could witness her like this, or run for shelter. He'd take his chances on Gigi.

"When can I start?" She flung the question at him.

He crossed his arms over his chest, causing his muscles to bulge. He leaned back in the chair so that the front two legs left the floor as he marveled at her. "Tomorrow too soon for you? We open at eleven."

"I'll be there." Gigi gave him a curt nod before turning on her heel and marching to the bar.

Roman watched with fascination as she stood at the bar, drumming her fingers while she waited. When she had the barkeep's attention, she muttered her order. He placed a shot glass on the counter in front of her and filled the glass with pink tequila. She slid a bill across the counter, picked up the glass, tossed it back, and then slammed it back down.

Something got under her skin. That was for damn sure. Roman gave Declan a sidelong glance as the bartender refilled Gigi's glass. Declan raised one eyebrow in question and nodded his head towards where she stood. Yeah, he wanted to know too.

The crack of the chair legs as Roman brought them down and stood got lost in the chatter of the bar. By the time he reached her, she'd slammed the second shot.

"Slow down there. You're gonna make yourself sick chugging your girly tequila like that." He closed his hand over her shot glass. "Something bothering you?"

Gigi took a deep breath, her back ramrod straight and her arms rigid at her sides with her phone gripped tight. "I needed to wash a bad taste out of my mouth."

His eyebrows shot up. He didn't know what to expect but that hadn't been it. "I promise you, working at the shop won't be that bad."

"I didn't mean that." Gigi bit her bottom lip as if forcing back a smile. She turned towards Roman, giving him an appraising look like he was a side of beef. Her voice was flat. "Tequila isn't really helping. It's too bad you'd get me into trouble."

He slid the glass away from her. Yeah, he was cutting her off. "I don't think you should drive. Can I give you a lift home?"

She waved him off, but whatever storm had been in her eyes had clearly blown through. Now her expression appeared vacant as her gaze meandered around the bar, looking everywhere but at him. Then her phone pinged and her shoulders came up rigid once more. She glanced down, and like that, the storm returned.

"I'll be fine. I live within walking distance actually." Her stiff posture and clipped tone screamed that she was anything but fine.

Whoever was on that phone had to be driving her mood. "Let me walk you then."

Gigi opened her mouth to answer but was cut off by her phone pinging. Her knuckles turned white as she gripped it. He'd put money down that if she hadn't been standing in front of him, her phone would have been flying across the bar—her agitation was that apparent.

"Sure. I'm going to hell anyway."

The text messages started ten minutes after she left her parents' house. She had been five blocks from the bar when the first ping taunted her. She wanted to know what trick Chad played to get that past her father. John Duval did not allow phones at the dinner table and these messages were not PG-13. The last message had her accepting Roman's offer to walk her home.

> DICK PIC: Take your panties off princess. Meet me at Red Barron.

That was immediately followed by a second text from Chad that made her want another shot and the nearest escape route.

> I want you bare under that skirt when I get there.

That had to be the shortest dinner her parents had ever put on, unless Chad begged off for an emergency and the emergency was her. Just the thought sent a chill down her spine that had Roman giving her a funny look.

She needed to leave this bar now.

Roman leaned across the counter and waved at the bartender. "Close my tab for the night."

After another minute, the barkeep was handing him back his card. Roman pushed through the crowd, opening her a path to follow. The regulars had been sparse when she first arrived but now with the hour growing late, things were starting to pick up. Maybe it had been longer than she thought. Whatever—the shots weren't affecting her that much and she knew her limit. She hadn't reached it with fruit-flavored tequila.

"So, do you own anything other than white t-shirts and jeans?" Gigi asked as Roman led her towards the door.

His hand grazed the small of her back. God, she felt that to her toes.

"Do you own something other than pink? Even the tequila you were drinking was pink."

That dragged an involuntary peal of laughter from her. She glared up at his golden eyes and the easy smile that made her want to pet his scruffy five o'clock shadow. God, what would that feel like against her skin?

He reached around her to open the door allowing the cool evening breeze to hit her. She almost groaned when she caught the scent of his cologne. It smelled earthy and yet fresh, like clean cotton but richer—spicier if that was such a thing. Whatever it was, she wanted to grab hold of his shirt and just smell him. Would his skin be salty or sweet? She was dying to taste him. Her senses ran in overdrive for this man.

"Which way?" His voice pulled her out of her smutty thoughts.

She pointed left towards C Street. What had they

been talking about before she'd been sucked into her sensory daydream? Oh, those yummy shots she'd been slamming.

"Don't knock it," Gigi said at last, trying to sound normal. "Tequila Rose tastes like a strawberry crème saver and goes down smooth." *Just like I do.* The words were on the tip of her tongue, but she was keeping them to herself. Ann would be proud.

"Are you one of those girls that only drinks the cutesy fruit drinks? Not that there's anything wrong with it..." She bristled at the laughter in his tone.

Grabbing his hand, she crossed the street, and then turned at the corner and crossed again, cutting into a small parking lot.

"This is me," she said gesturing at the building they approached.

Her two-story building reminded her of an Americanized version of a European villa, complete with fake balconies across the second floor windows and stucco exterior. The first floor contained storefronts and off to the side a green arched door served as the tenant entrance.

"Those cutesy ones are sneaky." Gigi leaned against the doorframe and looked up into his eyes. "The sugar hides the hardness beneath until it's too late and you're already drunk."

Roman braced one hand over Gigi's head and

leaned in towards her, his voice an intimate whisper. "Does that describe you too? Are you sweet to hide the hardness under the surface?"

His lips were so close. She licked hers and his eyes seemed to focus on her small movement. How was she supposed to not kiss him? That hooded look and his scent made him a magnetic force drawing out that needy part of her. He wasn't her boss yet. Would one kiss be so damning? It wouldn't qualify for the book she'd promised Ann to keep him out of. But then, she rarely stopped with just a kiss.

His golden eyes were searching, asking for permission. A fucking gentleman. Somehow, that made him sexier.

"Taste me and find out."

His eyes widened with her whispered dare. For a second she thought he would back off. Her need flared brighter with that banked amber fire in his eyes.

Roman leaned in, his lips brushing hers, testing. His eyes never left hers. It amped her need up another notch. That teasing touch made her throb. That he watched it all added to the lure. She liked to lead but this slow seduction had her enthralled and her panties ruined.

"Goodnight, Gigi." The whisper was a purr against her lips.

She blinked in surprise. That was it? The

hottest moment she'd felt in months and he just stopped? The confusion must have shown on her face because he smiled. Not a cocky grin, but a promise. Oh shit—what did that mean? He pushed off the doorframe and stepped back. Tomorrow he would be against the rules. She wanted him now.

"Roman—wait." She reached out, laying her hand against his chest.

His heart raced beneath her hand making her breath catch. He felt it too.

"You're right, sweet hits you harder than you expect." His smile was soft but he turned away, calling back over his shoulder, "See you tomorrow."

Gigi covered her lips with her fingertips as if she could hold in that moment. This was too good for the book. He'd be in a book all his own if he kept this up.

A horn honked and she jumped, the intrusion breaking the spell that Roman's lips had started. She opened the door and scurried inside, rushing up the stairs. Dick Pic was still out there looking for her. He might even have seen her.

She could never be with a man like Chad—now categorized as a onetime mistake. What about a man like Roman? Could she have him for more than her usual no-strings arrangement? Maybe she should thank Ann for that promise after all. Kissing Roman

Bishop would be playing with fire. A bigger part of her than she liked wanted to burn that particular candle all night.

# chapter 5

igi flicked on the closet light, casting a dull glow on her wardrobe and across her bare toes. Flipping through the hangers full of her everyday costumes, she dismissed her burgundy sweater and an emerald patterned blazer along with an assortment of understated button downs. None of them reflected her. They were the skin for the image she cultivated, a façade crafted to protect her privacy as much as her heart. Today called for a piece of the truth. Wholesome office professional with her bright but tasteful colors would stand out in all the wrong ways in this new setting. Her new employer had an edge and a challenge for her image.

She pulled out a formfitting magenta t-shirt dress from the back, tossing it on the bed with a couple other options. She could wear a color other than pink, but where would the fun be in that? Now that Roman pointed it out, she couldn't help the urge to meet his expectation. She certainly owned enough variations of the color to keep the silly game going for a while. If she couldn't have him, she'd settle for subtle flirtation until she lost interest. *Please let that be sooner rather than later.*

The garments had landed in a heap on her unmade bed. Arms crossed over her breasts, Gigi glowered down at her picks, considering them against the muted backdrop of her gray blanket and dusty mauve duvet. Sweet and unsullied struck her as the wrong message to be sending if she wanted to fit in or do any kind of flirting with Roman. That immediately ruled out the lacy blush dress. Also, the button down with white and pink polka dots came across scandalous with the amount of cleavage she would need to hide. That left the first dress she'd pulled.

She snatched the garment off the bed and held it across her body, petting the soft material as she turned to the narrow mirror beside the bathroom door. "Is this pink enough for you, Roman?" Her voice sounded hollow against the barren walls. "At least I'll be comfortable."

This dress stood in the reserves of her *me time,*

when there'd be no one to judge. Casual and bright but nice enough for a mall run or the store. This past spring, with a pair of sunglasses and strappy sandals, she'd worn it to the Czech Museum. She'd felt perfectly safe to do so. No one she knew would have been interested in the art exhibit.

Gigi slipped the garment on, smoothing the bunched fabric down over her hips, and then turned in the mirror to assess the results. There was nothing risqué about the dress. It covered her arms to her elbows and her legs to her knees. It was just bright and comfortable—the only flirty thing about it was the way the soft t-shirt material clung to her curves. It reminded her of her younger self, in high school where despite her father's disapproval she'd been free to be as bright and trendy as she pleased. With her denim moto jacket, this struck the balance of casual and professional she needed. High-heeled ankle boots and a leather cuff bracelet gave the ensemble the edge she'd been looking for.

The magenta and denim in her clothing made her stand out in the washed out grays, muted mauves, and blush pinks of her bedroom. She imagined the normal vibrant colors had been frosted and the cheer frozen from it. Unlike the rest of her apartment, it remained bare and she spent as little time in it as possible. Even the furniture choices were straight contemporary lines. The only pieces of art she'd hung over her bed to try to reclaim the space matched the drab palate. In the end, she gave up on this room.

If a man came inside her apartment, a rare occurrence, he was just as likely to take her on the velvet green sofa in her living room. There she could let her mind drift off into the rainbow of colors from the art collection she lovingly stacked on her bright white walls. When she'd finished with him, he'd be back out the door before he had time to find the bedroom.

Gigi grabbed her bag off the counter along with her tote carrying the items she'd need for her first day on the job. Only a quick jaunt across the bridge from Czech Village where she lived to the NewBo District across the river had her stepping back out of the car to work.

She used her sweaty palms to smooth down her dress one last time. Gripping her pink travel mug, she took a deep breath to calm her treacherous nerves. *This is just a job*. If she focused on that, maybe she could forget about the hot boss. This certainly wasn't her dream job—okay maybe the gallery part of it was even if she could do without the tattoo shop.

Since graduating, she had been floating from one stuffy cubicle and spreadsheet nightmare of employment to another. The gallery side of Ink Spinners would be her first shot at combining both her minor and her major. She needed to make this shot count if she wanted to leverage her career in a direction that was more her and less her parents' choices. If Roman had bothered to read her resume before offering her the position, he might have noticed. She minored in art history. Not exactly the ideal course of study to go along with business administration.

She grabbed her bag out of the back seat before marching up the sidewalk to get the day started. Roman stood behind the window turning on the neon open sign as she entered the shop. His golden eyes met hers with a welcome smile. Her lips tingled with the memory of last night. She shut the feeling down fast. If she planned to make it through this successfully, she would need to pack those feelings up and forget where she hid them. *Stick to the rules.*

"I'm ready to get started." Gigi sat her mug on the counter and turned on her bright cheerful smile— totally fake, but considering her last two days, forced is what she had to offer. "Do you have a back room for staff personal items or do I just keep my bag under the front desk?"

Roman leaned against the counter beside her, one foot crossed at the ankle, totally at ease. "Under the front desk is fine. The artists all have their own stations, but if you need to you can keep things in my office in the back."

"Thanks, so are we starting with a rundown on

how this place operates? What's the plan?" She pulled out a pink leather folder with a legal pad inside, also pink, and her favorite rose gold pen. Was her use of the color excessive? Absolutely. She also didn't care.

His eyes flickered over her color coordinated office supplies. His mouth—with those delectable lips that she totally should not be thinking about—quirked up into a smile. "There isn't much of a tour. You've already seen the gallery; there is an office, supply room, and bathroom straight back."

Her eyebrows shot up. Okaaaaay. She supposed she could wander to the back later. "So, then I guess you should show me your appointment keeping system."

"Sure." Roman moved around the side of the counter, opened the center desk drawer and pulled a calendar book out. Tossing it on the counter in front of her, he flipped it open to the current week. "Just write them in with the artist's name beside it on the date the client asks for. It's the artist's responsibility to check what they have coming up."

Gigi, stood frozen, pen poised for instruction. It dawned on her that she should probably close her gaping mouth—she shouldn't be rude on the first day. Her jaw snapped shut and she lowered herself into the desk chair behind the counter. It was amazing they could function like this. Once they became busier the system would break down—it lacked any kind of efficiency.

"What do you do with the computer then?" Surely, they were using it.

He shrugged. "Keeping the books and researching art references. Now that you're here, you can use it to set up our website."

"What about social media?"

"I'm not on it."

She swallowed hard and through force of will alone managed to keep her jaw from hitting the desk a second time. How could he run a business without social media? Even the President was on Twitter and that man remained stuck in another decade.

"I don't want to overstep. It's one thing for the shop to cultivate an image of the past. That's good branding. It's another thing to operate as if the century never turned. That's not good business." She gestured at the antique oddities that surrounded them as she made her point. "Please tell me that you and the other artists at least have smart phones?"

Running his hand through his slicked back hair, Roman chuckled. "We're not total savages." His grin had her sighing with relief, which set him to laughing again. "You have free rein to make whatever changes you think will make this place better."

"First, you need social media. I am happy to set it

all up and maintain it for the shop along with the website. It's really a vital marketing tool now. Also, I think I can do better for scheduling then a calendar book. When I'm done you'll be able to check your appointments from your phone."

"Cool, you need anything from me?"

"Art." Her answer was flat.

He cocked his head to the side, his expression thoughtful. "Art. I can do that. In the meantime I thought we could have dinner and get to know each other better. Does tonight work for you?"

"No." She worked to keep her voice flat and unemotional. She continued as if he hadn't just asked her out. "I have a concept for the website in mind, but it will require some drawings from each artist, especially you and Declan since you're the owners."

His eyebrows shot up in surprise and his answering nod was slow. She could see the wheels turning before he gave her another question. "I'm sure we can help you out. I'll talk to the guys. Anything in particular?"

"Just something that showcases the individual artistic style of each artist. Each of you will have a feature page where potential clients can check out your work."

Roman straightened and crossed the room to what Gigi assumed was his workstation. He tore a page from a spiral bound book that lay open on an antique barbershop chair, complete with aged black leather and intricate scrollwork. He laid the page face down in front of her.

"You can use this to get started." His cheeks were flushed and his hands were shoved into the pockets of his worn denim. "I'll be in my office in the back when my client gets here. Just holler."

For the third time since she came in the door, she gaped at him. At least this time it was too his back and the finest ass to grace a pair of jeans that she'd had the pleasure of ogling for the second day in a row. She hated when someone dismissed her questions, but she could stand him walking away when given a view like that. She swiveled the chair back to face the desk. Just what was the drawing that had him so—it took her a minute to sort through just what she thought he was feeling—embarrassed? Really?

Gigi lifted the corner, stopped and took a deep breath to brace herself. Curiosity had her fingers itchy, but the emotions rolling off him made her hesitate. This meant something to him.

When she couldn't stand it anymore, she flipped the page as if she was peeling a Band-Aid. Better to get it over with fast. Her breath caught as her fingers moved over the intricate line work and color. A pinup girl in a soft pink baby doll top knelt on a bed of darker pink roses, dark hair cascading over one shoulder. The stylized version of her own face stared back at Gigi. Her expression and wide green eyes were somehow secretive, amplifying the sexy pose.

Oh. My. God.

Trembling fingers moved to her parted lips. Her stomach flooded with giddiness and the skin on the back of her neck tingled as if Roman were watching her. She looked back over her shoulder as casually as she could manage, but if he was there, she didn't see him. If this attraction had been a war, between that almost kiss last night and this sketch today, his opening shots were brilliant.

It was as if he knew that the innocent act was just that—a mask, and he was right. He didn't know her well enough to see that. Yet somehow, he had. He captured it and presented it to her in full color. How did she even respond? That fluttering in her stomach had moved lower, igniting a smoldering need. She wanted to lock his office door behind her and taste what his lips had promised last night.

Artists were a sexy, dangerous lot. This one appeared to know her colors.

The bell on the front door chimed to announce a customer, cutting off the direction of her thoughts. Gigi tore her eyes from the artwork in front of her and met the smiling face of Ann, a Styrofoam coffee cup clutched in each hand. The lust that had been coursing through Gigi snuffed out instantly.

A forced smile spread across her face as she pulled the calendar over the drawing. Nothing suspicious about that, was there? The fluttering soured into a dull ache. She was such a shitty friend. Ann had all but handed Gigi this job on the promise that Roman wouldn't be added to the little pink book. It hadn't even been twenty-four hours and Gigi was nearly ready to break every rule—over a MAN. What had gotten into her?

"You're not Roman's first client today are you?" Gigi struggled to keep her voice even, to give nothing away.

Ann sat the coffee on the counter and waved her question away, appearing oblivious to Gigi's attempt to disguise her distress. "Of course not. Just wanted to stop by and visit you on your first day." She glanced around the shop before leaning forward and whispering. "Declan's not here right?"

Well now. That was interesting. Ann's eyes were wide as she fiddled with the top button of her blouse. Her seemingly unflappable friend had a chink in her armor. Gigi never would have expected it to be a tattooed looker, not with the guys she typically dated.

"No. I haven't seen him yet." Gigi flipped to the correct page in the calendar, giving her a more legitimate reason to cover the illicit art beneath it. She skimmed the lines until she came to his name. "Says he's not due in for another hour."

Ann's smile brightened. Her composure beginning to return. "Good. I brought you coffee and

I thought I might visit for a bit."

That sounded fantastic. All she wanted to do was unload this emotional mess on Ann. Her friend would know exactly what to think of Roman's actions if he had been any other man—but he was her step brother—the man Gigi promised not to fool around with.

Her phone chose that moment to ping from her bag.

"Is Dick Pic still bothering you?" Ann leaned casually against the counter, trusting and openly curious.

Gigi never thought she'd be grateful for one of Chad's messages. Now here she was, in need of a safe man problem to chat about and he delivered one just in time.

"The plot thickens." Gigi looked back over her shoulder, making sure Roman was still safely in his office before continuing. She kept her voice low and her tone matter of fact, despite the agitation she felt. "His name is Chad and he works for my father. He was their guest for dinner when I showed up. He tried to shove his hand in my panties under the table and followed me into the bathroom for a quickie."

Now it was Ann picking her jaw up off the floor. "He didn't."

"He did. I braved the wrath of Dad and got out."

Ann pointed an accusing finger at Gigi. "This is what I warned you would happen if you kept messing around. You need to settle into an adult relationship."

"I'm not that kind of girl." Even if Roman tempted her—Gigi wouldn't be admitting that.

Ann huffed and then pursed her lips in one of those *I know better than you* smirks. It was as if Ann was playing a game of cards and counting to make certain she beat the house. "We'll see about that."

Gigi's brows shot up. "All I know is, I'm steering clear of my dating apps and regular hookups for a little while until this settles down."

"In that case, I'd like this guy's number so I can thank him."

Gigi tossed her pen at Ann. "Get out of here. I have work to get done."

Ann smirked again as she backed towards the glass door with her own coffee in hand. "Have fun pulling my brother out of the social media dark ages."

"You knew?" Gigi's voice went up an octave in frustrated shock as she threw her hands up.

Ann stood with her hip holding the door open. "Of course I did." She ducked out, her laughter cutting off as the door closed behind her.

That bitch knew everything. Good thing she was on Gigi's side—at least until catching her lusting after

Roman. Then all bets were off.

Roman focused on the lines of ink flowing through the machine vibrating in his hand. His art kept his mind from wandering and he sorely needed that especially after this morning. He didn't mean to listen in. He'd just wanted to see her reaction to his art—to her likeness from his pen. He needed something after she'd turned down his dinner invite so flatly. Talk about unexpected, especially after that hot teasing kiss the night before. Between that and the conversation he eavesdropped on, he was all kinds of twisted up. For a moment, her seeing his art had given him hope.

It wasn't a bad reaction. She didn't storm out or threaten to sue him for sexual harassment on the first day. Yeah, now that he thought about it—that could have gone very badly. Instead, she was a buzz of activity, taking pictures of the shop on her phone and each of the artists as they came in. As absorbing as his work could be, there never came a moment when he hadn't been viscerally aware of her presence.

"Damn man—the view in here got a serious

upgrade." The gruff proclamation from Roman's long-standing client, Billy Joyce, had Roman lifting his needle to look from the half sleeve to see what she'd done now to inspire this observation.

It wasn't even a question that by "view" Billy was referring to Gigi. She sat reclining in the office chair, one foot tucked underneath her and her shoe dangling from the toes of her other. But it was the way she worried her full bottom lip as she worked at the computer that made him want to beat his chest like a possessive cave man. He'd never been that kind of man before and at this stage had no right to be now. How could he have it this bad for a woman he'd only known a couple of days?

He shook his head and sighed before refocusing on his client. "Mind your manners, Billy."

"Don't worry man; I'm too old to be poaching on another man's territory."

Roman lifted the needle again and raised a questioning eyebrow, but didn't speak. Billy had been a friend of his father's from his "glory days" as they liked to refer to their military experience. After Roman's father passed, Billy had offered his body up as a canvas in the early days of Roman's apprenticeship. Now as payback, Roman covered up the amateur flash art with new, better work. They did one every few months. Naturally, Billy had occasion to voice his opinions a little freely.

Billy chuckled as he rubbed his buzz cut. "Yeah,

man, it's that obvious. Every time you stop, or she laughs, speaks, anything—you look at her. It ain't taken you this long to finish me up since you were an apprentice. She's gonna think you're a creep if you don't knock that shit off."

"Then I guess it's a damn good thing you're my last client for the day." The phone rang and she picked it up. Roman took advantage of her distraction to continue candidly. "I happened to hear the lady doesn't do relationships and I don't do casual."

Billy waved it off. "You're just gun shy after that cheatin' hussy you were with before. You're lookin' for excuses to let her get away, son."

Roman glanced up at Gigi for the hundredth time that day. Her head cocked towards them, but the phone was pressed between her cheek and shoulder as she tapped on the computer. He didn't need her hearing about his past from someone else.

He could admit that the conversation he'd eavesdropped on had made him pump the breaks. That didn't make him gun shy. It made him evolved. He learned from his past mistakes instead of repeating them with a new pretty face. His instinct told him she was more complex a creature than his ex had ever pretended to be. It drew him to Gigi—made him want to find out the why behind the things she said instead of cutting his losses.

"Not gun shy, Billy. I'm building the support beams to break down a few walls."

"Glad to hear it." He smirked, baring crooked teeth that looked more like a snarl than a smile if Roman hadn't known that grizzled face for so long. "You about done? I'm tired of sittin' still."

Roman sprayed and wiped the excess ink from the image he'd etched into the right bicep. Today's piece had a nautical theme, featuring a mermaid and a ship with full sails in an American Traditional style. It seemed like a lot to fit in one tattoo but they'd managed and the result was impressive even by Roman's standards.

Billy got up and ambled his hulking frame to the mirror to check out his arm. "Damn, man. I think this is my best one now."

"Mr. Joyce," Gigi cut in, using her honey tone rather than the clipped professional one she'd been dishing out since Ann left. "Can I take a picture of your art for the website?"

Roman turned so that she couldn't see his face and mumbled to Billy, "Be nice."

"Shut your trap, Roman. I know how to talk to a lady." The old man shot him a scathing look before grinning at Gigi. "Of course I wouldn't mind."

Her smile brightened and she snapped a couple quick photos, offered her thanks, and then returned promptly to the desk. Roman covered the tattoo to protect it and then cashed Billy out.

"See you later at the bar."

"Pull the trigger, kid."

Roman waved him off and the older man chuckled as he ambled out the door.

"Mr. Joyce is nice. I have to say your clients have been quite the surprise."

"What do you mean?"

"I mean that today I've watched a man in a suit come in and roll up expensive dress shirt sleeves to get your work, then Mr. Joyce, who is old enough to be my father. But the math teacher earlier—she took the cake. I never would have thought someone like her would have ink."

"You hang art in your house, right?"

"Yeah, but this isn't the same," Gigi shot back.

"Your body is the temple for your soul. Why shouldn't it be reflected in art just like your house?"

"That's pretty deep stuff."

Roman shrugged. "I'm an artist, not an idiot."

"Never thought you were. It's just that it's so philosophical."

"I've got hidden depths. Which is why you should let me take you to dinner and show you." She said no earlier and sure, it had bruised his ego— but call him a glutton for punishment because he just couldn't let it go, no matter what his reservations might be.

She stilled beside him and turned, facing him fully. Her cheeks flushed and her green eyes burned bright. But the downturn of her pretty pink lips gave him his answer before she did. "Roman, you're my boss now. I don't think we should."

Roman searched her expression for any hope. No—her expression was kind but stern so he saved face the only way he could think of. He changed the subject despite the bullet of rejection burning in his chest. Screw Billy and his fucking trigger. "Anyway, it's late and you stayed longer than you needed to. Why don't you take off and I'll close up shop."

Gigi bent to grab her bag from under the desk. Roman struggled to keep his eyes fixed on the money he counted and not on her heart shaped ass. He choked down his disappointment, carefully keeping his expression blank as she straightened. The air felt thick between them—damn—she even smelled like the flowers he'd used as a background in the pinup art.

The soft lilt of her voice broke the trance he'd been standing in. "I know I just started today but if it's alright with you, can I start planning the first gallery event?"

He shoved the cash in the bank bag. There was no use counting it tonight. He couldn't even think right now, knowing they were alone, and in that intoxicating cloud of her perfume after she'd shot him down. "I'm wide open for Saturdays evenings. Book it whenever and let me know."

Moving around the counter hesitantly, she backed towards the door and then leaned against the glass as if waiting for something. She opened her mouth to speak and then closed it.

Roman gripped the counter hard, just as he had when she first walked into his shop. "You have a nice night. See you Tuesday."

Gigi sighed heavily and shook her head. "Yeah, see you Tuesday."

orking at a tattoo shop had made for an interesting week, and certainly more fulfilling than any Gigi had ever spent in cubical hell. The tattooed hunks she worked with treated her with more respect than the stuffy professionals strangled to death by ridiculous neckties. She'd long held the theory a necktie kept the blood flow restricted to their dicks instead of their actual brains.

Of the five artists working here, not one of them had even attempted a pass at her or gotten flirty—including Roman after she shot down his request for a date. It was as if some kind of professional switch had flipped. After that beautiful drawing he'd given her, and the mixed signals of his on again and now off again flirting, they currently stood on radio silence. It had her all mixed up. Sure, she asked for the end of their mutual flirtation, but she missed it.

Gigi spun around in her office chair, pulling her long sweater closed as she crossed her arms over her chest. Roman sat with one leg tucked beneath him. His ever-present white tee hung half tucked into dark washed jeans, cuffed at the ankle. She even liked his boots with their ridiculous red laces. The supple leather appeared worn and the color was mottled and weather-beaten. It reminded her of the golden brown char of a toasted marshmallow if you didn't burn it to black. Of course that brought to mind campfires and being curled up in front of one.

To be clear, she was not the kind of girl who went camping. However, she could do a cabin and a bearskin rug for the right man. She was nearly convinced that this rugged and sexy object of her temptation was the right kind of man for just that. He cleared his throat and her gaze shot up to meet his as he glanced up from the girl who lay prone in front of him. Their eyes met and he smiled before returning to the girl's tramp stamp.

Gigi studied his dark hair, messy from when he'd been jamming his fingers in it earlier while he'd been drawing up the tattoo design he was laying down now. She imagined he'd be similarly mussed after a tumble in her bed. As she pictured it, the thick black frames of his glasses slid down his nose. Something else she never thought she would find sexy. She'd learned that he needed them when he was drawing or tattooing a client. His dark eyes sparked with interest over the top rim of the frames as he alternated between his work and watching her.

The corners of his lips quirked up, leaving her practically panting to kiss that damn dimple and feel the scruff of the day's stubble against her soft skin. She licked her lips and his smile spread. She'd been busted.

It was utterly inconceivable that she should be sitting here fantasizing about her boss that practically oozed hot and nerdy instead of doing something about it—or more to the point—doing him. She could lie and blame her self-imposed dry spell for wanting Roman this bad, but she'd want him even if she'd been serviced by one of her gentleman friends on her lunch break. She needed to lose Chad in a bad way before she did something reckless and stupid to jeopardize this job.

"You want to take a look?" Roman lifted the tattoo gun and wiped his work clean. "I'm assuming that's what you're so curious about."

Not really, but then she'd have to admit she was checking him out and not his art. She plastered on a pleasant smile and nodded as she uncoiled herself from her seat. Moving around behind him, Gigi swept the bulky weight of her dark hair off to one side to prevent it from touching the client or him as she leaned over his shoulder to look.

The girl's denim and her white lace thong had been pushed down just far enough to reveal the upper half of her bare ass, making Gigi's cheeks heat with jealousy. Even if she did take exception to the cliché placement and the way he'd had to become intimately acquainted with his client's anatomy to complete it, the work itself was exceptional.

An intricate crown and script that read "royal" in bold letters served as the centerpiece but it fanned out on each side like crystal strands of a chandelier. It flowed with the curve of the client's ass, dipping down low.

"It's beautiful." Gigi hadn't considered that a tattoo could look so delicate. She actually had to stop herself from the urge to trace the fine lines with her finger. "It looks like jewelry."

Roman's smile broadened at the awe in her voice.

The client squealed happily. "I am so excited to see it now."

"Does it hurt?" Girls like Gigi—or rather the kind of girl she pretended to be—didn't get ink, but that didn't mean she couldn't be curious.

The client peered over her shoulder at Gigi. "Sometimes, but mostly I just zone out to the buzz of the needle and after a while it just feels numb, like someone left a vibrator on my skin for too long."

"You thinking of going under the needle, beautiful?" Roman's soft words spoken in a low gravel tone, just for her ears, felt like a caress in places meant to be touched in private.

Her own answer came out breathy to match. "No, but if I did I would love that chandelier look."

Gigi stepped back, returning to her post at the counter and his attention returned to the woman spread out before him. Something pretty from his hands would be nice—a secret just for her—a peep show into the woman that lay beneath the public persona. She found the thought appealing. She imagined being naked under his hands while he left a permanent mark on her body in the form of art, the pain being soothed away under his touch. Would he kiss her and make it better? The wicked thought—low level though it was—made her smile and she filed it for later fantasy consideration.

The heat and soft pressure of Roman's hand pressing between her shoulder blades woke her from the haze of her own imagination before his voice registered. "Have a nice night, Dolly. Stop back if you have any problems." He looked down at Gigi as the door closed softly. "Looks like it's just you and me again tonight. What's that make—third time this week that you and I were the last two here?"

Gigi hadn't meant to stay so late but she also couldn't stand to leave him alone with that pretty blonde client and her beautiful tramp stamp. Pot, kettle, black—don't care. "I was hoping to show you your new website. I didn't want to interrupt you with your clients just for that." That sounded like a reasonable enough excuse. Bonus points for not painting herself as a jealous shrew.

He quirked an eyebrow up as if to say he wasn't fooled but she tilted her chin up defiantly. His answer made her wish she hadn't opened her mouth. "Show and tell could be fun."

She swallowed hard as she pictured his eyes on her while they took turns in a slow strip tease. That sounded so much more fun than a graphic design reveal. A wistful sigh escaped her lips before she could push it back down where it belonged. And from the grin that was quickly spreading across his lips, he heard it. Maybe that flirty switch could be turned back on after all.

He leaned against the counter, arms crossed over his chest mimicking her own closed off posture. On him, with the colorful ink on his skin and the slight bulge of his flexed muscles, it was sinfully hot, making her flushed as she once again suppressed urges that were off limits for this man.

Roman know it wasn't fair to tease her. In fact, he'd been a perfect gentleman all week, but it was wearing him down. The way she fucked him with her eyes nearly had him on his knees begging to taste her. He suppressed a groan at the thought.

When she walked in this morning wearing another pink tunic over skintight leggings, he'd become painfully aware of her. If she hadn't covered her foxy little self in that chunky white sweater, he might have had to kick the boys from the shop because he wasn't sure his jealousy could handle it. She wet her full lips painted the same shade of pink as her top and his eyes were instantly locked in. He wanted his hands buried in the tumbling mahogany waves of her hair as he took those lips, claiming them with his own. Hard or soft didn't matter to him. But it was gonna be more than that teasing taste from the week before when he'd left her at the door like the gentleman his mother had raised him to be. He wasn't feeling like a gentleman tonight.

He pushed off the counter and walked to the window. He turned off the neon sign and then moved to the door, softly turning the lock. She watched him with rabid interest as he moved back to her. He could see her calculating each action, as color flooded her cheeks.

"If I were to lay ink on your body, where would you want my mark?" He'd caught her paying special attention to the tattoos that the shop's female clientele came for, measuring each woman as a threat—or not— and then reconciling the woman with whatever design she chose. She wanted it. She just had to warm to the idea and if he had anything to say about it, she'd be getting her art from him only. He couldn't stand the thought of another man's hands on her naked flesh.

"Someplace hidden—just for me. I saw a picture on Pinterest of a woman that had it underneath her breasts. I thought that was pretty." She looked up at him though her dark lashes.

He leaned against the counter beside her again. His legs crossed at the ankle while he let his mind drift to the kind of image he'd create for her. Soft pink roses came to mind first but she'd said she liked the jeweled look of Dolly's art. He would enjoy letting his mind spin on that for a while.

"That would be fitting on you." His voice came out a little rough with the lust that was riding him hard. He had to remember why he couldn't touch her. He needed a reminder right fucking now.

She cleared her throat and pointed at the computer monitor. "I've got the web page. Do you want to navigate it or do you want me to flip through the pages for you quickly?"

Blessed reality saved his dick just in time. His girl was all business because she didn't do relationships. That's what she'd said while talking to Ann right after he'd given Gigi that pinup art. That's why he couldn't have her. He forced an affable smile, dialing back the smolder with a little more ease now.

A copper metallic header came up on the screen

for Ink Spinners Tattoo & Gallery. The background was a collage of black and gray photos of the inside of the shop, proudly displaying the collection of gears and antique medical oddities that he and Declan obsessively curated over a lifetime. A box told the viewer about the idea behind the shop and a schedule of events. The next tab she went to was for the gallery. The skull made of layered gears had been featured front and center. The header declared the gallery's opening night on the following Saturday.

The next six pages were for each artist. The background for each created from a different black and white sketch provided by the featured artist. It contained a color image of the artist, a bio and two links. The first link took you to the artist's portfolio. The other link took you to a scheduling page, complete with a form so the artist would have a heads up on what to expect.

It hadn't escaped his notice that on Roman's page she hadn't used the sketch he'd given her, but he let that go. He didn't really want it on display anyway. It had been something intimate for the two of them and he'd only given it to her in an irrational need to offer her a glimpse into what he wanted with her—a glimpse she hadn't mentioned once.

"You really did a great job capturing the feel of this shop and each artist, Gigi."

She beamed with pride at his praise. That satisfied smile had him wanting her all over again.

Would one more taste of her be so bad? If he took the leap and she didn't stop him he wasn't sure where it would end or if he wanted it to. If she would just give him some sign that he wouldn't be crossing a line this would all be so much simpler.

"I've got some ideas for the setup for next Saturday I'd like to show you as long as you have more time," Gigi said as she rose from her seat. She walked backwards towards the gallery, her eyes locked with Roman's, pulling him along after her like he was caught in a tractor beam. "This gallery opening is already pulling big numbers on the Facebook event post I set up."

His voice dropped to a suggestive growl. "I'll make as much time as you need."

Her business smile turned sultry, telling him she'd picked up on his double meaning. This was the side of Gigi he liked—the vixen who was sure of her own needs—not that prim businesswoman who tried to play innocent. He felt that look burn through his blood as it all rushed into his erection. Her smile cranked up another notch. Yeah—she noticed. He couldn't imagine much carnal knowledge getting past her.

"I think we need a bar. Not a huge selection. Maybe just two choices. Something geared more towards the ladies and something more towards the men. Definitely classic in keeping with the place."

"Rosé for the ladies and whiskey for the men."

And yes, the Rosé was because it reminded him of her. He was already pathetic.

"That's going to get a little pricey," she said in a low teasing voice. She stopped in a dark corner of the gallery where an antique chaise lounge had been pushed up against the wall. "I think this would be the perfect place to set the bar up. Do you know anyone who could be our bartender? We can't charge for the alcohol unless we want to get a liquor license for the event or hire a caterer that has one."

"You've been doing your homework."

She lowered herself onto the chaise, and perched on the edge with her hands gripping her knees. "You never asked, but I double majored in art history and business. Pissed my parents right off. When Ann sent me here, she knew the gallery side of this would be too good for me to pass up."

"You love art." Learning pieces of her like this made him want her so much more. She was right, if he had read her resume or asked a single question that first day, he might have already known. "I feel like I missed an opportunity to learn so much about you. Do over on the interview?"

Gigi laughed. "That ship has sailed. You're going to have to get it the hard way now."

"Dinner?" He moved closer to her, mesmerized by her soft smile and the way her hair moved in the dim light as she shook her head.

"You're the boss now, Roman. I think dinner

might be against the rules. Don't you?"

He shouldn't be surprised that she'd feed him the same argument—but still the tension between them had made him hope.

"Not my rules." He prowled towards her, until she had to crane her neck back to look at him. "Couldn't you quit for the night? I'll rehire you tomorrow."

Her sudden laughter held an intoxicating glimmer of her as she tossed her head back and abandoned herself to whatever joy she'd found in his silly declaration. In that unreserved reaction, he could see moments of a future that right now stood only as a tempting mirage. Images of shared secrets and jokes under the covers on a lazy Sunday morning, or tickling as he chased her through the halls of a museum where they should behave. The tantalizing image of what a real life could be with her beyond the shop, beyond the epic sex he knew they could have, rocked him—and hardened his resolve to keep trying.

Without meaning to or thinking about it, his gruff hands cradled her face, thumbs tracing her full bottom lip as her laughter stilled. Her tongue darted out and grazed his thumb. His emotions were all over the place. He'd gone from intense need to professional distance and back to need again. If he was being honest, when he was with her the need always hovered just under the surface of all their interactions.

This could go so wrong—the errant thought made him hesitate. He needed her to cross the last hurdle.

He wanted her but just as she said, he was still her boss and her best friend's brother—not that any of it bothered him or would stop him. If it mattered to her, then she needed to be the one to decide. For the sake of his own heart that had been smashed when he once thought he had everything, he needed to know she was all in with him.

He handed her the control and when her eyes widened he knew that she knew. He felt her little fingers curl into the waistband of his jeans and she used it to pull him down on his knees between her spread thighs. For the most painfully slow moment of his life, she stared back at him, waiting or testing. He had no idea which. As long as she kissed him, he didn't really give a fuck.

"Screw it. I'm going down happy." The words were a groan and there was no time to process what she meant because her lips were on his and he had his green light.

She tasted like the cherry cola she'd been sipping on all day. It was his new favorite soda because on her it was fucking amazing. This was not the soft and sweet taste they'd had before. The longing burning in his gut since that night drove him to claim her mouth with bruising force. When she opened up to groan her approval, he let his tongue delve deep. She met him, stroking his questing tongue with her own—and damn if that didn't crank him up more.

As if that wasn't enough, her hands were making

him crazy. She'd run her sly little fingers up the inside of his shirt and alternated between teasing light touches and grazing his ribs and back. With a gasp, he pulled back for air and a little sanity. She whimpered as they parted and that little sound jacked him up— just like everything else about her.

"Roman—please don't stop."

Had kissing ever been this hot—had anything? They weren't even into the heavy petting yet. If she was game, it was time that changed. He ran wet, teasing kisses along her jaw, and worked his way down to her neck.

"Not yet, beautiful," he promised between kisses that he wished would brand both her skin and soul as his. "I'm only stopping if you want me to."

She moved her hands to his face, drawing him back to her welcoming and now kiss-swollen lips.

Roman moved his hands up the outside of her spread thighs, stroking the soft material of her leggings. He continued moving his hands north to her hips and up the soft plain of her stomach. When his thumbs grazed the lace of her bra through the material of her shirt, he stopped his progress. She was having none of that. Arching into his hand, she moaned her approval as he palmed one breast and then the other, slowing the frantic pace they'd started.

Every one of her lush curves felt like perfection in his hands, making his cock ache for more. If he wanted this to be more than just tonight, he was going to have to walk a fine line. He needed to find the sweet spot between a fling with the boss that she'd regret and craving another touch. She was such a wild card and he didn't like games—just her.

Roman pulled back from their kiss, resting his forehead on hers. "I don't want to rush this. You're worth more than that, but damn if I'm not hungry."

"Just a little more then." Her voice was a hoarse whisper, reflecting the longing that raged inside of him. "Please, just a little more."

He stared into the green fire of her pleading eyes. It reminded him of absinthe in a crystal glass through the filter of candlelight. Specific as that was, he'd had that thought ever since the moment he first looked into her penetrating gaze. Their ability to intoxicate him exceeded the power of the green fairy. He knew he should stop right here, but if she wanted more, did he really have the will power to deny her anything?

Gigi gripped his white shirt. She turned on the chaise, reclining back and pulling him with her so that he lay pressed against her, cradled between her open thighs. He braced one hand on the seat to keep his full weight from crushing her. Then she rocked her hips up, the heat of her sex scorching his hard cock through all their fabric barriers. This hitch in her breath as she rubbed herself against him, working herself over—just damn. He simply didn't have the words for the answering fire it drove in him, but if she was going to cum it wasn't going to be from dry humping. He wanted to control that release. Needed to be the reason she found her pleasure—not just a tool she used to get off.

"I want to touch you, beautiful." He was asking a lot considering they'd only just opened the flood gates with their first real kiss, but she was a woman in firm control of her sexuality. If anyone could handle his request, it was Gigi. Her demanding little hips were practically begging him for it now.

Her lips spread into a soft yet teasing smile. "Yes, please."

Roman took her mouth; this time he took her slow and deep. There was no need for the frantic rush between them right now. He shifted his weight out to the side, leaving the cradle of her thighs. His right hand began the teasing glide down her body. He let it trail downward across still covered breasts and her soft tummy with a feathery touch.

She raised her hips and with one hand attacked the leggings that stood as a barrier between his touch and her body. He smiled against her lips as she struggled and kicked the fabric between them until she was free.

When he lifted his lips from hers and looked down the length of her body, his satisfied smile spread. She had kicked her flats to the floor and her leggings lay in a heap on top of them. She was beautiful from her pink polished toes up the curve of her calves and thighs, to the white lace panties still hiding her sex. Her right leg bent up at the knee, pressed against him as he lay with his back to the wall. Her other leg dangled over the edge of the chaise.

He slipped his hand inside her panties, cupping her hot sex. Gigi bucked against his hand and moaned as he inserted one long finger, stroking slowly to spread her silky wetness.

"Is this where you want me?"

She tightened around his finger, answering with her body. When she relaxed again, he added a second, pumping slow and easy. He pulled out of her and stroked upward, pressing flat against her swollen clit. He rubbed the engorged bundle of nerves in lazy circles before moving down again to slip back inside her. He alternated back and forth like this, picking up the pace slightly with each pass until he found a rhythm that had her moaning and bucking beneath his hand.

"Roman." He loved his name on her lips. Her voice was whining, pleading with him to finish her without actually saying the words.

"I've got you, beautiful. Just a little bit more."

He curled the two fingers pumping inside of her up, to find that spot, the internal nerve center that would drive her pleasure higher. He knew when he'd found it because her sex clamped down around him, demanding him not to move. When he began working her clit with the pad of his thumb, she came undone.

The nails of her right hand dug into his shoulder

where she gripped him as her hips bucked and her sex pulsed around his fingers. She bit down on her plump pink lip, holding herself back as she groaned loudly. Watching her cum was the most beautiful art he'd ever made. Damn if he didn't want to do it all again, until she didn't hold herself back, until she screamed her pleasure as uninhibited as her earlier laughter had been.

Not tonight.

As the pulses slowed, the tension in her body bled out and she went limp under his touch. Gently he pulled his fingers from her soft folds and her now ruined panties.

"Now can I take you to dinner?"

Gigi's laughter was immediate and without reserve. "Yes, Roman. After the way you played me, you can have anything you want. Better hurry up and take advantage."

"Dinner's enough for now."

chapter 7

how could anyone resist something this intense? Gigi hoped Ann would understand because it had been a foolish promise from the onset. She hadn't meant to kiss him in the gallery or the insane orgasm he'd given her afterword, surrounded by the artwork he'd created. Gigi's rules were a flimsy fortification at best in the face of their ongoing flirtation; they may as well have been straw because he was the big bad wolf.

She only meant to flirt before continuing with gentle resistance. She also didn't regret that it happened and wouldn't let him either. She owned her actions without shame or hesitation. She had since the first liberating fling. Roman would be no different, at least not that way. The need to prove that fact had her sitting across from him in this little restaurant sharing a piece of lemon cream cake. Another rule bites the dust—dinner dates and sex did not go together when you don't do relationships. Her date might get the wrong idea.

Hours of shared laughter and life stories over a bottle of wine and divine pasta had gone a long way towards lighting up the darkened corners of her soul. When she met up with her gentleman callers, it was sex and nothing else. No dinner after or talking softly while holding hands. Right now, her left hand stretched out across the table, his fingers entwined with hers—another broken rule for the tally. Was this what relationships were supposed to be like? If so, she could become addicted. Which was exactly why she should put the brakes on whether she wanted to or not, before it was too late. That was the whole point of the rules.

"Penny for your thoughts?" His low words and dark eyes burned across the candlelit table between them with warmth and a hint of concern.

She offered him a thin smile and a spoonful of cake, which he claimed from her with a deliberate slowness that felt like a sensual promise. "This is nice, being with you like this." She couldn't quite keep the breathy note of longing from her voice, but she gave it a valiant effort.

"This isn't the only date I'm ever taking you on."

She looked away and he reached out, turning her face back towards his so that his dark eyes could probe hers. "We don't have to label this yet."

Still, there were things he deserved to know. "I might seem like it, but I'm not the kind of girl you take home. You see that, right. You see past the front and the limit that puts on us?"

Roman was quiet, just looking back at her. His expression was openly appraising. So much so that his gaze was more like a physical touch, gliding across her cheek and then her open collar, searching out the small bare pieces of her. She held perfectly still, allowing him to take his fill while she siphoned off her open pleasure from the visual caress. It took the edge off the needling voice her anxiety raised over this newness.

"I see that it limits you." His voice was low and somehow challenging without losing the gentle persuasion that got her this far. "I see you. Not the things you've done. I'm not interested in that. Just interested in you."

Her shoulders slumped with relief. His head tilted and his eyes narrowed in thought or confusion at her reaction. She didn't want to worry him, not yet. She wanted to enjoy him just a little longer. It wasn't fair but she was ultimately a creature selfish with her pleasures.

Wisely, he changed the subject to safer ground and he slid his cash into the black leather folder for the check. "Tell me about your name. It's unique like you. So I'm sure there has to be a story there."

They rose from the table and he helped her with her coat before they walked to the door. The restaurant they'd chosen was in easy walking distance to her place. It was enough to make her steps drag to prolong the evening.

The stars were bright in the cloudless ink overhead. Even the glow from the street lamps couldn't hide all of the tiny pinpricks of light. She lifted her face to the sky, soaking them in as Roman slipped an arm around her waist. Instantly she felt his warmth chasing away the slight chill in the air. It may be uncommonly warm for March, but enough bite remained to remind you spring may be coming but it wasn't here yet.

"You still haven't answered me." He prompted as they started down the sidewalk.

Gigi leaned her head against his shoulder. "There's a little something to it," she admitted at last. "My mother loves all things French. Her favorite movie is *Gigi*. It's about a young French woman who falls in love with a wealthy family friend. She transforms herself so they can be together. Only he doesn't like what she turns herself into. He loves her for who she's always been."

"That's beautiful, like you." He whispered it against her temple and placed a soft kiss there.

She shrugged. "I wish my name was something

more normal like my brother John Jr."

Roman stopped and grabbed her arm, spinning her to face him. "Gigi, you're special and your name reflects that. Nothing else would have fit. I think your mother knew exactly what she was doing."

How did a heart not melt with words like that? It couldn't. She was in so much trouble.

The kiss that went with that declaration was reverent and soft even as it built in intensity. When he pulled back, she was dizzy with the intoxicating scent of his aftershave and the swirling hormones he'd sent buzzing through her system all over again. He pulled her back into his side and she was blinking in confusion as they resumed their walk to her place. She was still in a daze when she realized they were standing in front of her building.

Oh god—was he going to kiss her again. She really hoped he would kiss her again.

Would everyday be like this if they were together for real? She could see dinners and dates at the art history museum. Snuggling in bed late in the morning. She would cook him breakfast and they'd make love in the shower. Were these things he would want too? She needed all of that with a sudden wave of intensity that left her reeling. She never dreamed of anything like this. It had never been in the cards of her imagined anything, but now it wouldn't stop playing on repeat in her mind's eye. She could burn her little book for a man like

Roman. She could do it only for Roman.

Gigi leaned against the doorframe, as she had the other night. He held her like a woman and not like a toy. She hadn't known there would be a difference until he showed her tonight. She liked it. Roman braced a hand over her head and brought his lips crashing down on hers, stealing a moan from low in her throat. God, the things this man made her feel. Warm slick need already spread through her core, further adding to the ruin of her favorite pair of lace panties.

He pulled back, leaning his forehead against hers. Already it turned into a familiar gesture—one she enjoyed. Perhaps like her, he needed a break from the thing building between them but couldn't stand to sever contact.

"Goodnight, Gigi."

"It doesn't have to end here," she whispered, her pulse racing with the urges he kept bringing to life inside of her. "You could come upstairs."

Roman groaned. His face contorted in a wince of pain. "God, I'd love that, but not tonight."

Now it was her turn to groan in pain. God, her pussy already ached with need. He hadn't even gotten off when he'd played her body earlier. She couldn't imagine why he'd deny them both like this.

"I know, beautiful, but I told you I don't want to rush this more than I already have."

He took her lips again in a burning kiss as he

moved to shield the view of her body from the street. He reached between them, cupping her sex, rubbing her through the thin material of her leggings. Her already primed body, flush with need and the denial he'd flung up between them, shuddered immediately with the contact. Dear god—he'd brought her to an immediate climax, fully clothed, right there on the goddamned street, swallowing her scream of pleasure with his kiss.

It barely took the edge off.

"Better now, baby?" he asked as he laid teasing kisses along her jaw.

Her own question came out breathless as she tried and failed not to pant like a bitch in heat under his ministration. "What about you?"

Roman leaned back, smiling that sexy leer at her. "I'm a big boy. I can take care of myself."

"I don't doubt that. But I want to take care of you."

He stepped back from her as he took his hands off her body. "Then you have something to look forward to on our next date."

"Sneaky bastard," she muttered as he started back up the sidewalk away from her.

His deep laughter split the night but he kept right on walking.

This evening went so sideways. Gigi sighed and let herself into the building before dashing up the stairs to her second floor apartment. Her keys were in the door when her phone dinged with an incoming message. She smiled. He couldn't even make it home before he messaged her. She pushed the door open and stepped inside. Let him sweat it out a minute.

She kicked the door closed behind her and shucked her jacket, letting it drape haphazardly on one of the magenta pink club chairs. Yes pink—no doubt Roman would have had a laugh about that if he'd come up. That assumed he'd have a chance to look. A smile tugged at the corners of her lips as she dropped into the emerald green sofa.

This was her fun room and her bright furniture her first adult purchase. Her apartment should have been the one place she could pull back the curtain and be totally unreserved. She held her ground—mostly. Her mother decorated the bedroom—the polar opposite Iceland—as a gift. Really it was a direct response to her father's appalled reaction to the way Gigi had done her living room. They'd dropped by unexpectedly and the next thing she knew boxes from West Elm started showing up. Another not so subtle attempt to direct her life in the direction her father felt most appropriate.

Gigi's head lolled back against the cushions, arms flung out wide, with her feet up on the walnut coffee table. Her mind wandered into the happy randomness in the odd gallery arrangement of paintings climbing every bare wall in her living room. It wasn't random.

Not really. The logic behind it had more to do with the unseen, the reason she chose those pieces over so many other options. This was her happy place. Her art. She'd gone so far as to paint her walls a brighter white than the basic that the landlord had done, to better highlight her collection. The result being a bright wave of colors large and small to make her smile—her adult version of an infant's mobile—a vibrant distraction.

The washed out red windmill against a Parisian night sky drew Gigi's eye—the water color that started her passion for art. A vacation to Paris at fifteen, her mother's favorite city, changed the course of her life. There had been the usual tourist bait of the Eiffel Tower and the Arc de Triomphe—fine, fine but boring. When the artist spun tales of the can-can dancers and courtesans, her interest sparked. The discovery of the story hidden inside those pictures—the meaning—sparked her curiosity at a time when cheerleading tryouts and who was taking who to spring formal absorbed her world view. Thanks to that little old man with his toothless smile, she'd walked into the Louvre with an open mind. It had been a bonus that her father had been horrified she purchased a painting of the Moulin Rouge.

The irony was not lost on her that her first piece of art depicted an upscale brothel masquerading as a dance revue, while her life was a performance designed to hide, using an assumed role to hide that she liked sex and to hide from love behind that sex. She could even draw comparisons between the dance hall and Ink Spinners. So many layers, like paint, overlapped to create the full story. Most of her gathered pieces were like that—street vendor art with hidden depth.

The phone pinged again and her smile spread. Maybe, she should call Roman back—invite him up. Or maybe a little tease over the phone, something to let him have his satisfaction. He'd taken care of her so thoroughly. She was down with whatever. Pulling a pillow into her lap, she hugged it to her chest and rifled through her purse with her free hand. She held up her phone and scanned the waiting text.

Dick Pic: Need to Talk. 10 Min at Red Barron.

Not Roman. The ice bucket challenge just dropped on her right there in her living room. The smile fell from her lips. Shit. Ignoring Dick Pic clearly wasn't working.

Chad hadn't stopped messaging her since dinner at her parent's house. Most of the messages had been mildly pornographic. Thankfully, none of them were threatening. He would suggest they meet and she would never show. He'd try sexting or sending her videos of himself jacking off. She always told him no or asked him to stop in her responses. Then she saved it all. If this got any worse, she'd have to get a restraining order and she'd need evidence. She didn't want it to come to that.

Now, it was time for a stronger approach. Good thing he'd picked a fairly public place. She stepped back out the door, relocked it, and then started towards the bar where she'd first asked him to pick her up over two weeks ago.

Despite the stalker boy toy and the epically awful sex, she'd met Roman. He was wonderful enough to make up for the shit show this joker wouldn't stop putting her through. The one evening of non-sex she was having with Roman made all her other sexual experiences pale in comparison.

Yeah, she had to get rid of Chad fast. She didn't know how this thing with Roman would play out or what she wanted from it. Chad could ruin it all if she let him. She wasn't going to let him. She picked up her pace on the sidewalk and hoped to God that Roman hadn't decided to come down here for a drink. This would be a bad time to run into him.

She stepped into the dimly lit bar. She liked it for its anonymity and the fact that she could walk there made it simpler to leave with her gentleman callers. It was a standard place as bars went, with the neon liquor signs, dark spaces and the pool tables one expects from such dives. On first glance, she didn't look like she belonged. Few would guess she was more comfortable in her skin here than any swanky piano bar or urban nightclub others might expect her to frequent—not that she gave many people the chance to know this or anything else about her.

Chad waited at the corner of the bar facing the door. His eyes were dark and cold with anger. He dressed as if he'd come here straight from the office in dress slacks and a chambray dress shirt. He waited with rolled up shirtsleeves and his collar hanging open with his tie loose as if he pulled it to relieve the pressure at his throat. He'd planted his long legs wide as he leaned against the barstool.

Gigi approached with her chin up and shoulders back. She wouldn't go into this confrontation meek because it was clear that's what this was going to be. His own stance was combative and simmering with anger, probably from the way she'd been ignoring him.

As expected, he wasted no time calling her to task. His hand shot out gripping her arm and pulling her into his body. He spoke through gritted teeth. "Is that jerk you were kissin' the reason you've been ignoring my messages?"

Jerking her arm free, Gigi took a step back from him and his breath that was rancid with the stench of stale beer. "The man I was kissing is none of your business. I've been answering your messages by telling you I'm not interested. I have been perfectly clear each time I answered."

"I'm not taking no for an answer. Your father wants to see us together," he said as he reached for her again.

Gigi sidestepped his touch. "I'm not interested in what he has planned for me. I'm my own woman. Not a doll for him to arrange a life for."

His sneer was nasty, showing the vile human being she'd suspected he kept hidden under his skin. "How about I tell Daddy just what you've been up too?"

If she could spit fire, she would have. If she caved to his demands now, she'd never be rid of him. As much as she hated the idea of her family or anyone else knowing about her nocturnal activities, she'd rather that than let any part of this piece of trash touch her again. "You wouldn't dare, not with so many of your own skeletons to keep. I swear I need to shower in disinfectant after touching your filth."

"You like it dirty. Don't pretend you don't." Chad reached out again and this time she wasn't fast enough to avoid him as he grabbed her by the pussy.

Her hand snapped out and cracked him across the face. His hand fell away and every eye in the bar stopped to stare at her as she came unhinged. "You do not have my permission to touch me." She turned on her heel and marched away.

"Gigi, wait." Chad pleaded but stayed in his

seat.

"Don't contact me. I mean it." She called over her shoulder, but she didn't stop moving or turn back around. She practically sprinted home, afraid Dick Pic would follow her. She'd have to stop calling him that. It sounded too cutesy for someone ballsy enough to grab a woman like that in front of half the bar.

chapter 8

igi didn't feel safe until she was behind the deadbolt on her apartment door. She felt dirty. And damn it—he ruined her post orgasmic high.

The phone in her bag dinged frantically and she was sure he was bombarding her with messages. Probably trying to get her to come back or worse, threatening her if she didn't. She would not rise to it. She would not be bending for him or any other fool. How do you go back to chopped steak once you had Grade-A prime-cut beefcake? You don't.

She wasn't fully convinced she was ready for a relationship with a man like Roman, but there was zero chance of having one with Chad. Men like him were the reason she didn't do relationships. She would not end up like her mother—not for any man. Which led her back around to Roman. She shouldn't have taken the leap with him. It wasn't fair since she was being so indecisive still. On the same token, it was done and she couldn't put him back on a shelf.

Once again, she was in dire need of her best friend to help navigate these waters. Unfortunately, that was something else to feel guilty over. She promised Ann that she wouldn't fool around with Roman. She lasted all of two weeks before she was coming apart in his hands literally and figuratively.

Gigi collapsed on her sofa. She dug the offending phone from her bag and tossed the purse to the ground at her feet. Cradling it in her lap, she stared down at the green and white speech bubble icon and the red circle with its number thirteen, taunting her. *Ding.* Correction, fourteen.

She pulled her chunky sweater tighter around her shoulders as if it was armor and dialed Ann. She couldn't tell her best friend everything but she'd at least know what to do about Chad or offer a shoulder to cry on. Not that the asshat deserved her tears.

It rang twice before Ann's brisk cheerfulness came on the line. "Gigi? How's it going? I've been seeing the buzz about the gallery event next Saturday. I knew you'd do right by my brother."

That was Ann, sidestepping the personal and rushing straight to business talk before you could answer her first question. Gigi felt a stab of guilt at just how "right" she'd done Ann's brother. Ann had trusted her and now Gigi rewarded that faith with secrets and half-truths.

"The gallery opening is coming along nicely. But that's not why I called." Gigi choked back a sob. "Things are getting worse with Chad. He messaged me tonight that he wanted to talk. I met up with him so I could tell him in person to leave me alone."

"Tell me you went someplace public." Her words came out in a rush of concern.

"Of course. But he grabbed me." Her hands shook as she told Ann the rest of the story, leaving out that he'd seen her kissing Roman and maybe more.

When she finished the line was silent. She could hear Ann breathing so she knew she hadn't lost signal. Gigi stood and began pacing the hardwood floors that ran the length of her open floor plan living space. "You're freaking me out here, Ann."

"I'm sorry I'm just...shocked is the word I'm looking for. I mean I always thought your boy toys were eventually going to lead to trouble." Gigi hated being called out with an *I told you so*. Ann had never made it a secret that she disapproved of Gigi's lifestyle but she rarely held it against her or made her feel bad for it. "No matter what I think, you don't deserve trouble. You're not doing anything wrong, not really."

"There isn't anything wrong with having a healthy appetite for sex and not waiting for prince charming to make you feel good." Gigi voice came out more defensive than she'd meant but she firmly believed there was no shame in the life she'd been leading and when she wanted a better one she would change, like she was starting to do with Roman. In the meantime, she made no apologies.

"I'm sorry. I don't mean to raise your hackles because you aren't wrong."

It did not escape Gigi's notice that Ann didn't say she was right either.

"I think you should start carrying pepper spray and maybe think about a restraining order."

"I've thought about the restraining order too. He's left me at least fourteen messages since I walked out of that bar. I've been saving them all for just that reason. But he is a lawyer and knows my father so I'm just not ready to take that step."

"Will you at least have my brother walk you to your car at night?"

"Yeah, I can do that." That would be happening anyway and probably a lot more for reasons Ann didn't need to know.

Oh no—what if Roman told Ann about what they'd started? There was nothing Gigi could do to stop him that wouldn't raise his suspicions about why. She'd have to press her luck.

"Thanks for letting me vent, Ann. I'm sorry I snapped at you a little."

Gigi padded into the bathroom and cranked on the hot water. It suddenly sounded like a fantastic idea to wash off the stain of Chad's violating touch. She only wanted to remember the parts of the day with Roman in them. She sat on the edge of the tub in her tiny apartment bathroom and tested the water, tempering it with cold until it was just right.

"I get it. I'm here anytime you need." Ann hesitated as if she meant to say something else.

For a moment, Gigi wondered if Ann knew there was something Gigi was leaving out, but Gigi wasn't brave enough to pursue it.

"You have a good night," Ann said at last.

This week with Gigi had been more than Roman could have hoped for. He was a romantic fool. Sitting in his office watching her like he was now, he worried a little. Gigi had been more than attentive to him when they were alone. What concerned him was her preoccupation with her cell phone. When she checked the frequent pings she chewed her bottom lip in an expression he'd learned meant something bothered her. Other times her eyes blazed with fury when she focused on it. Whenever she caught Roman watching, she smiled sweetly. Something was wrong there. Something she wanted to hide.

His sister's cryptic phone call hadn't helped either. His mind drifted back to the too brief conversation with Ann, mining it for clues that Gigi had yet to be forthcoming with.

"Roman, I need you to do me a favor because our girl Gigi isn't going to ask." Ann usually came across high-strung, but now the clipped tremor of her voice practically screamed trouble.

"What's wrong?" His voice deepened with concern.

"I can't tell you if she hasn't, but I just need to be sure you walk her to her car at night and watch out for her whenever you guys are out together. I know you see her at Red Barron sometimes."

So, Gigi hadn't told Ann about them. That was okay, he wouldn't mess with their friendship by spilling it now. It did make him wonder why she would hold that back. Seemed Gigi wasn't all in despite her claims.

"You don't have to worry, Ann. I'll take good care of your friend." It was an easy promise to keep since he planned to spend as much time together after hours as he could wrangle out of Gigi. She seemed a little averse to relationship

basics like dinner dates.

"I know you will. That's why I called. Trouble is, she doesn't always take good care of herself. That's all I'm going to say. She'll murder me if she knows I talked to you about this."

"No worries. I won't say anything."

He hadn't said anything since they hung up that call. Now, watching Gigi, he had to wonder if the problem came from whoever messaged her on the other end of that cell phone.

The only thing easing Roman's mind after that was the girl herself. Gigi always had a smile for him and when he walked her to her car at night, she sank into his kisses, hot and pliant, begging him to follow her home. He wasn't ready and neither was she. He needed to know she was committed to this, committed to them.

Roman leaned back in his chair as Gigi sauntered into his office. She closed the door with a soft click before crossing the tight space. Stepping between his knees, she leaned her ass against the desk behind her. A full color mental image of her bent over that desk with her ass in the air had him adjusting himself.

He looked up at her, his gaze hooded. "What's up, beautiful?"

"Just wanted to get your approval on a couple last minute details for the gallery event tomorrow night. Your next client isn't for another thirty minutes so I thought now might be a good time."

Roman sat forward, wrapping his arms around her waist. "Make it fast because I can think of a better way to use that time."

She chuckled softly as she used her slender little fingers under his chin to tilt his head back to look up at her. "I'm sure you can, but let's keep things professional while we're here, shall we? You can always follow me home later."

He huffed like a petulant child but stayed quiet, allowing her to get on with her business.

"I called around and it turns out our favorite drinking hole, the Red Barron, would be happy to step up tomorrow with their liquor license and serve your requested rosé and whiskey. I was able to rent a bar and the necessary glassware from the local event company, although if we do enough of these we might think of purchasing our own at some point. I've emailed you the quote, so if you could just pay the bill we'll be all set."

"If you emailed me you didn't need to come and tell me. I think you came in here for something else, a happier distraction maybe?"

She laughed and pushed him, sending the chair rolling backwards. "Don't flatter yourself. I know how you are." She reached behind her and grabbed his sketchbook, waving the evidence like a flag. "You're here sketching, not checking you emails, and I need that bill paid today."

She tossed the sketchpad back down and pushed off the desk, turning to leave. She got one hand on the door before she stopped and looked over her shoulder. Her voice was soft and the corner of her mouth turned up flirtatiously. "I bought something special to wear tomorrow night. I was hoping at the end of the night you'd come home with me so that I can show you."

Maybe she was ready. It also occurred to him that if he kept telling her no, then eventually she'd lose interest or think he had. It couldn't be further from the truth. He wanted her so bad on his best day that he had trouble breathing when she was in the room whether her intoxicating green eyes were on him or not.

"Tomorrow can't get here fast enough," he answered at last.

Her smile sparked brighter and then she slipped out the door.

chapter 9

igi had been planning this event since the first moment she walked into this shop and knew this job could be hers for the taking. Now the gallery show was here and she was almost sorry—not sorry—that she wanted it over with as soon as politely possible. It was utterly selfish of her to think like that. This event meant so much to Roman and Declan. It would be the making of the gallery side of their business.

She blamed Roman. With every stolen moment making out with Roman like a teenager, her need climbed to dizzying heights that no man had ever drawn from her. Tonight was going to be the night. No rule or promise would hold her back after the long teasing game he'd played all week. He fingered her as if she was a sixteen-year-old virgin for fuck's sake and she begged for it!

Was this love? She didn't know. What she did know was that every conversation or shared laughter, every secret look, brought her closer to that elusive feeling. She had never even imagined it could be this way or that she would like it this much. She might burn in purgatory for breaking her word to her best friend, but she'd burn with a smile because so far, it had all been worth every broken rule.

Gigi turned sideways in the shop's full-length mirror. They kept it in the back outside Roman's office for the clients to better view their magnificent body art and it offered her a little privacy to finish her preening. She assessed the black beaded dress that she'd chosen because it reminded her of the fancy flapper dresses from the roaring twenties, then leaned in to slick on her Moxie Mauve lip shimmer.

She'd pulled out all the bells and whistles for tonight. If she was doing this monogamous relationship thing, she was doing it right—including new lingerie. She couldn't explain it, but it mattered that this first time at least, he would be the only man to ever see her in this set. In fact, she was strongly considering burning everything she had and replacing it.

"Wow. Is all that for me?" The deep timber of his

voice was reverent as he slipped up behind her and laid a chaste kiss on the curve of her throat where her pulse fluttered. "You look stunning, but where is your pink, beautiful?"

His hands skimmed down her sides until they came to rest on her hips. She covered his roving hands with hers and smiled. "That's a secret for you to find later."

"Damn, Gigi."

She barely had the chance to enjoy the hard evidence of his appreciation pressed into her ass before he was spinning her around. Their lips collided in a savage kiss that stole her breath and, for a moment, the strength in her knees as he walked her back until the press of cold glass met the exposed skin visible from the low back of her dress. One hand slid from her ass to her knee, drawing it up. His other hand buried in her curls. She'd worn them down and messy just for this reason. She loved the feeling of him possessing her like this, hot and brutal. She didn't even mind that she was gonna have to reapply that lipstick. This kiss was worth the extra effort.

"I don't know if I'm going to last until later. You're making me want to take you in the office and lock the door." The growl of his voice whispered into her ear sent a sensual shiver down her spine that made her want to rub her thighs together to relieve her sudden surge of need.

He pressed kisses along her neck that made her burn with weakness, but he'd denied her for days and it was time he had a taste of his own medicine. "Down, boy. You can wait, just like I did." Her voice was shaky, but she was proud of herself anyway.

His chuckle turned into a groan as she pushed him back gently with one hand braced against his chest. And damn—he looked nerd hot now that she was getting a better look at him. He'd slicked back his hair with pomade and worn a white button down shirt with the sleeves rolled up his thickly corded forearms, keeping his colorful ink on full display. At his throat, he'd opted for a navy and teal bow tie which she thought suited his vintage style right along with the suspenders that attached to his cuffed dark wash jeans. She almost laughed when she got to his boots with the lumberjack red laces.

The look was quirky and badass, but most of all, it was just him. She adored that he wasn't like other men. He marched just outside the beaten path and owned it with confidence that was sexier than any Armani suit he could have owned. As a couple, they probably looked odd together, as if they didn't fit. For the first time in a long time, she didn't care. For once, her carefully crafted image didn't factor in her decisions or her confidence.

Roman twined his fingers with hers. "Come on. I have something for you to try."

He pulled her out into the shop and into the

gallery without allowing her to fix her swollen lips. She grinned despite herself as he wove through the people starting to mill through the space. She blushed when she spotted the chaise where he'd brought her off just a few days before. He'd moved it in the center of the space so that it stood directly across from the painting she'd fallen in love with on that first gallery walk through, the painting with the man screaming on his knees. She'd since confirmed that Roman did paint that heartrending image. He continued back to their corner, right where she suggested they place the bar.

"Hey, Billy," Roman greeted the bartender and sometimes client. "Thanks for working this on such short notice. Was your supplier put out?"

Gigi smiled warmly at the older man. "You own the Red Barron? That explains so much."

"Not a problem at all. Besides when I heard you boys were doin' this and your honey of a manager was setting it up, I knew I couldn't let anybody else take care of ya. Another joint would have robbed you blind." He slapped a heavy hand on the bar top they'd brought in for the event and his deep belly laugh rumbled through the gathering crowd. "Roman's cooking up something special for you, girly."

The upturned curve of Roman's lips that he attempted to hide forced Gigi to suppress a smile of her own. If she didn't know better, she would have said he looked embarrassed about whatever he'd done. That only grew her anticipation.

Roman slipped behind the bar as Billy wandered off to talk to one of the servers they'd hired. He pulled out a silver bowl of sugar cubes, a crystal glass that he balanced a silver slotted spoon over and a fancy glass decanter filled with what looked like an herb green liquid. While she watched, he poured a shot of the green spirit into the glass, then placed a cube from the dish on the spoon and poured seltzer water slowly over the top, dissolving the sugar. The resulting mix clouded into a milky opalescence.

"*La fee verte*, the green fairy. The first time I saw your eyes they reminded me of absinthe. I thought maybe you should try it." Roman's crooked smile was proud as he handed her the beverage.

She raised the glass to her nose, and allowed the herbal bloom of the drink to wash over her senses. "I've heard of this. Isn't it illegal?"

Just the idea made her think of moonshine and speakeasies. An oddly romantic gesture that suited their unique courtship.

Roman shook his head. "Not any more in this country. Once upon a time it was banned all over Europe but France had the biggest hard on about it." He pointed at the crystal glass in her hand and started tucking away all the items he'd used behind the bar. "Try it, but be careful. That stuff's hundred proof. We won't be sharing that with our guests. It's a treat just for you."

The thought he must have put into this made her heart flutter as she raised the glass to her lips. The sweetness teased her tongue first and then it reminded her of licorice and herbal tea. It was a strange pairing, just as they were. She was instantly enamored with the cocktail. She moaned as she sipped her drink.

"Roman, I adore it. You should have some."

His smile brightened as he came around to stand beside her. "I'm glad you like it, but I'm gonna wait for now." He leaned into her side and whispered in her ear. "If I drink tonight, I might lose the control that's keeping me from throwing you over my shoulder and leaving right now."

Heat crept up her neck at his lust-filled words. God, she wanted this man. Loved the way he made love to her mind before he even touched her, engaging every part of her being. She had a feeling she would be addicted the second he filled her up with all of himself.

"Promises, promises," she muttered around a syrupy sweet smile.

He growled low, sending vibrations of air across her heated skin. "Don't tempt me." Then louder he announced, "Let's mingle."

Roman placed a hand at the small of her back. Shaking hands and greeting guests as they worked the room pressing flesh and encouraging sales. Gigi had worked out a smooth plan. Declan and one of the other artists waited at the reception counter, cashing out buyers and arranging for later pickup or delivery of the art, then someone tagged the piece sold, but it remained on the wall for guests to view. Some of the paintings had the option of limited edition prints for sale as well, something for everyone's budget. If all went well, the boys stood to rake in thousands in one evening, making the open bar a drop in the bucket.

Gigi happily sipped at her divine drink as she smiled and absorbed Roman's warmth.

Until Ann raced towards her with a panicked look on her face. "Ten o'clock. Daddy dearest is here and that arm candy doesn't look like your mother."

"Oh my god—he can't see me here." Gigi's answering whisper came out shrill. She caught sight of him and his surgically enhanced date. "That hussy is younger than me. What am I supposed to do?"

Ann's gaze locked onto Roman's hand at Gigi's waist. She frowned but said nothing. Ann took a deep breath and with her pragmatic efficiency launched into an on the fly plan. "Keep working Roman around the room and keep one eye on the cradle-robbing-bastard. Stay on the opposite side from him at all times. If you and Roman get separated you can stay hidden in the crowd behind your dad somewhere."

Ann started to move away but Gigi gripped her wrist to stop her. "Thank you."

"We'll discuss this later." Ann's curt nod toward Roman conveyed her meaning.

Gigi should have known better. She had been aware Ann wouldn't miss this but she'd allowed Roman to cloud her thoughts and paw all over her anyway. Now her father was here. This was going to be a disaster. She slammed what was left of her fragrant cocktail, allowing the warm buzz to ease through her. She was going to need another drink.

Tugging on Roman's hand, she waited for his attention then lifted her empty glass and shook it before gesturing with her head towards the bar. He let go of her hand and smiled before resuming his conversation.

She'd made it ten steps away from him, maybe fewer, when a hand on her gripped her ass that didn't feel like Roman's. She spun around and nearly toppled off her heels. As if this evening couldn't have been ruined any further, Chad leered down at her with his arm around some tarted up Tinder reject. He didn't stop and talk to Gigi—thank god for small mercies—just kept moving with his eyes locked on her. Like he was trying to rub his date in her face and make her jealous. Well, he was about to be disappointed because she shook her head and turned back to the bar and Billy with his magical green fairy drink.

Setting the glass on the bar, she batted her eyelashes at the jovial barkeep. "Think you could make me another of that divine concoction that Roman gave me? Pretty please."

Billy chuckled and started mixing her drink. "How can I tell you no when you ask me so sweetly? But you mind Roman's warning. These pack a punch, girly."

He slid the glass towards her and she picked it up, raising it in a salute. "I'm counting on it."

Turning back with her liquid prize in hand she kept to the edge of the room, carefully working back to Roman. She made it within ten feet before she stopped, frozen. Her father stood pointing to the painting she loved, sale tag in hand as he discussed it with his date and Gigi's boyfriend. Of all the places her father could have brought his little whore, why did it have to be this place? The only place with the one man that was starting to feel like home, and they're tainting it with their sin. Gigi slammed back her drink and immediately snatched a full glass of rosé off a server with a passing tray.

Her head swam with emotion as she knocked that glass back too. This night couldn't be any more ruined. Not with Chad circling her like a vengeful shark, her father lurking and oozing debauchery all over her happy place, and Ann promising retribution without saying a threatening word. She knew in the beginning she was going to burn in hell. Turns out she was doing it in an expensive dress.

The Ink Spinners Gallery opening event had been a resounding success, and Roman knew exactly how he wanted to thank Gigi—just as soon as he found her.

She'd disappeared when she went for her second drink. Workaholic that she tended to be, he imagined she'd run off to make sure things continued to run the perfect course she'd set in motion. What he imagined versus what she'd achieved by simply leveraging the social media that he'd been ignoring, staggered him. Now he was ready to make good on the promise and find that pink she'd hidden just for him.

Roman leaned against the bar as Billy packed away the rented glasses and unopened bottles of liquor. "Hey, have you seen Gigi? I lost track of her when she came back for her refill."

"No, man. I think she stuck to the rosé after her second drink, so I didn't really see much of her after that, not with the girls circling with drinks."

"I know where she is." Ann leaned against the bar beside him. His sister looked like a pillar of gold with her champagne cocktail dress and blonde hair pulled back neatly. She'd dressed to catch Declan's eye. She'd never admit it, but she didn't have to be here otherwise.

Roman turned to give his sister his undivided attention. There was something going on or she would have just told him where to find her.

"So that painting of the man on his knees?" She pointed to the one in front of the chaise.

Roman smiled. "Shame it sold. Gigi loves that one. I probably would have given it to her."

"You sold it to her father tonight."

Roman's face scrunched up as he thought through all the people he'd spoken with. "That older guy with the plastic-looking girlfriend?"

"That's the one." Ann's tone was clipped and devoid of any humor.

"Why didn't Gigi introduce me? Is she embarrassed of her stepmother? She shouldn't be. I mean if anyone knows about shitty stepfamilies, it's us." He punched Ann in the arm playfully but when she didn't laugh, that's when he started to worry.

"That's the problem. Gigi's parents aren't divorced."

"Oh shit." Roman leaned into the bar, rubbing his closed eyelids. "Where did she hide?"

"Your office and she's pretty inebriated right now. I can take her home."

Damn it—this night was supposed to be a celebration. He wanted it to be special for her. It had started out so well. "No. It should be me. I've got her from here."

"Do you? She's an emotional handful when she's been drinking, thanks to that hornet's nest she calls a family. If you break her heart..."

"Are you fucking kidding me right now?" He took a step back, palms out. "You know what, never mind. I know where she lives. I'll get her home safe. That's all you need to know."

Roman walked away, shaking his head. He must have misheard his sister because he couldn't believe that she actually doubted him, even for a moment. Gigi was hurting and no way would he ever take advantage of that vulnerability or allow anyone else to. Ann had no idea how precious this woman made herself to him already.

Gigi was right where Ann said he'd find her—curled up in his desk chair, cradling a bottle of wine in her lap. Her high heels lay scattered on the floor and her feet tucked under her. For a moment, he thought she had fallen asleep, but then she lifted the bottle to her lips and took a long pull.

"Oh, beautiful—that bad?" He pulled the bottle from her hands and sat it on the desk. "Let's get you home and tucked into bed."

She looked up at him with glassy eyes. "Figures. I finally get you to come home with me and I mess it up by getting drunk. You should find a different girl, Roman. A better one."

"Sorry, you're not getting rid of me that easy." He scooped up her shoes in one hand before guiding her arm around his neck. "Come on, stand up for me, babe."

Gigi groaned as she peeled herself out of the chair to stand on wobbly legs. She reached for the wine bottle he'd taken but he guided her just out of range. She did at least manage to grab her handbag as they weaved out the door and through the shop.

"Goodnight, guys," Roman called as he led her to the front door.

Isaac Hart, one of the newer artists who stayed to help cash people out, waved as they passed. Declan kept counting money and didn't bother to look up. Typical. They made it to Gigi's car without incident. He buckled her in on the passenger side of her Fiat and fished her keys from her purse. He'd have to leave his motorcycle here overnight because there was no way he was going to let her drive home like this so he could get it back to her place.

Gigi was quiet on the short drive. She stared blankly out the window at nothing or everything; he wasn't sure which because her face was completely vacant of the women he felt so much for.

This was the second time Roman seen Gigi hit the alcohol hard. Of course, she stopped early with the tequila. This time he had no idea how much wine she'd had. If she had asked to leave, he'd have taken her home, but then he also knew why she hadn't. She'd gone to so much trouble for that event. The last thing she would have wanted was to drag him into her nightmare. How often did Gigi suffer in silence to make others happy? He was also sure he wouldn't like the answer if he put the question to her.

He pulled into the closest space to her door that he could find. As soon as he shut the car off, she popped her seat belt and the door, leaning out with her head between her knees.

"Hang on, Gigi. I'm coming around to get you." He exited her little car and ran around to her side.

Gigi rolled her eyes to look up at him, her head still hanging. "I think I had too much. I'm so sorry." She sniffled and tears slipped down her cheeks. "I ruined everything."

Roman knelt beside her and tilted her face up to look him in the eyes. The pain radiating from her face broke his heart. "Beautiful, you didn't ruin a damn thing. Just let me take care of you and I promise tomorrow we'll get right back on track."

Gigi nodded slowly.

"Good, now tell me your apartment number and I'll get you up there."

She groaned and tried to stand, but he pushed her back down into the seat. "I'm on the second floor, 2B."

He lifted her arm and put it around his shoulder before threading his own arms behind her back and under her knees. He lifted her easily and, without prompting, she tightened her grip on his shoulders. Carefully, he pushed her car door closed and then crossed the parking lot to the exterior door of her building; with a little team work he got her in the building and up the stairs.

He set her down just long enough to unlock her door and then lifted her again. She giggled and he smiled down at her. "Straight face, beautiful. Dress rehearsal for your future role as Mrs. Bishop."

chapter 10

$g$igi stared at the glass of water and two aspirin waiting for her on the nightstand. A vague memory of strong hands and a deep voice coaxing her to drink a similar glass of water teased at the hazy edges of last night. She sat up gingerly and reached for the glass in hopes of rinsing the cottony nastiness from her mouth. This could have been so much worse. In fact, it should have been. She didn't even remember how she'd gotten home last night.

She shuffled to the bathroom to refill the glass. More water—that's what she needed if she wanted to keep dodging this hangover. She jammed a toothbrush in her nasty mouth, and then she caught sight of herself in the bathroom mirror. Holy hot mess. She still had on last night's dress and her mascara had run, leaving her eyes a smeared black smudge, like some kind of drunken bandit. Bonnie without her Clyde came to mind, considering the wannabe flapper dress. Her hair had turned into a tangled and wild mess. It would not have surprised her to find a fucking squirrel hidden in there.

Roman must be so disappointed in her right now—oh God—Roman. That's how she'd gotten home. What had she been thinking getting drunk like that? Instead of drowning herself in a pity party for one, she could have been having hot sex with the first man to tempt her into more than a casual fling. Whatever was happening between them was not going to be over after one night and for the first time, the idea appealed to her.

That also messed with her head.

Now she had to worry if he still wanted her AND face the wrath of Ann-- because there was no way Ann didn't know after the possessive way Roman was touching Gigi when Ann found them at the party. She might even have to go back to hunting for a job on Monday. With the way she'd acted, Gigi wasn't ruling it out.

Disgusted with herself, she scrubbed the offending makeup off her face, replaced it with the weekend minimum of fresh foundation and lip-gloss, and then took care of the usual morning necessities.

She padded back out into the bedroom ready to shed the dress for something more comfortable for her pity party. She made it as far as the dresser when the heavenly smell of bacon assaulted her senses.

She scrunched up her nose in confusion. "What is that?" Her stomach rumbled, impatient for the savory aroma wafting in from her kitchen.

Abandoning her quest for yoga pants, she poked her head out of the bedroom door. The stack of French toast cooling on her kitchen island caught her eye first and then Roman, half-naked flipping bacon in the skillet. Holy shit. Talk about taking your life into your own hands—grease burn anyone? Her gaze moved over the hard planes of his body, catching on the way his jeans hung low on his hips, giving her just a hint of the fine ass it contained.

Splatter bacon splatter. She totally planned to kiss any resulting burns to make them better. In fact, she should prove just how medicinal her tongue action could be. Or not. He was probably pissed about her behavior last night.

"Good morning." God, she hated that her voice betrayed her as shy and fucking meek. That wasn't her. Confident and brazen—that's how her voice should have come out. Instead the fear of losing him undermined her hard-won confidence.

Roman spun around and revealed the ridiculous frilly apron he'd dug out of her drawer to protect his skin. She was both disappointed and turned on. Pink floral and aqua polka dots never looked so sexy. He hadn't bothered to tie the back or she might have noticed it. Now she was going to get all hot and bothered every time she unearthed it to bake. There were worse problems to have.

He snaked one arm around her waist, pulling her flush against his hard body for a gentle kiss. "How's your head this morning, beautiful?"

Such a simple loving action. No judgement, no harsh words. He made her breakfast and asked how she felt. Fuck—she had to choke back tears.

"I'm fine." Her voice shook as she said it.

He looked at her with a slight frown. "Are you sure about that? Did you take the pills I set out for you?" She nodded weakly, and he continued. "Good. Grab a cup of coffee and have a seat while I make you a plate. How do you like your bacon?"

"Extra crispy," she mumbled.

Roman chuckled. "Good, because that's how I made it."

She had to be caught in a dream or some kind of altered reality brought on by that fairy drink he'd given her last night. Still, she wasn't about to argue. When she finished fixing her coffee, a plate sat waiting for her.

Stewing over her expectations and this new reality with Roman, Gigi poked at the scrambled eggs, pushing them around the plate. "I can't believe you did all this. I thought for sure you'd be gone this morning or at least angry at me."

Roman leaned back against the counter. He'd lost the apron and stood feet crossed at the ankle, nibbling like a mouse on a strip of bacon. "I see two problems with what you just said." He held up his fingers counting them off. "One, what kind of a man would I be if I didn't take care of my hungover girlfriend properly? For the record that does include aspirin and bacon."

"Don't forget French toast," Gigi mumbled as she swiped her finger through an errant drip of syrup.

"With a girlfriend named Gigi, it seemed like the natural choice."

Her hand stilled, hovering over her plate. "I'm your girlfriend?" Her heart fluttered wildly as she whispered the question. He said it twice. The first time she just thought he slipped. The second time seemed more deliberate.

He raised an eyebrow and ignored her question. "Two, why the fuck would I be mad at you?" He came around the edge of the counter, dropping the bacon on her plate as he turned the stool she perched on to face him; their noses almost touched. "Sometimes life leaves you no option but to numb the pain. If I had been paying attention, I could have done that for you without the alcohol. You went for the next best substitute. Although next time I suggest you use me instead."

His fingers curled around her wrist, as he drew her fingers up to his mouth. One at a time, he took each slender digit into his mouth, sucking the sugary liquid off as his eyes locked with hers. It was the single sexiest thing anyone had ever done to her that didn't involve actual sex. Damn.

Gigi wanted to pay attention to those words. She should be asking what he knew about why she'd been drinking. She just couldn't think past the building pressure between her thighs.

Roman leaned forward so that his lips grazed her ear. "We could talk about this or I could show you just how distracting I can be."

He took her earlobe between his teeth, teasing it with a gentle suck that stole an involuntary groan from her lips that sounded suspiciously like "please". Her skin burned wherever he touched her, aching to have him brand her body with his heat.

"And you're definitely my girlfriend." His voice was a low growl, staking his claim in a visceral way that should have bothered her.

Had Roman been any other man it would have sent her running. With him she wanted to be claimed and that too should have worried her—but god help her she wanted it. She wanted him to take her right here, bent over this counter. His lips teasing her neck had her panting for it.

She needed to get her head back in this game and remember herself. She needed control.

Yes, she started last night planning to have him, but her plans had been shattered. Last night had been her choice. This morning, this was something she hadn't planned, even if she was still wearing the pink lace set she'd purchased just for him. So much of their time together had been unplanned as she succumbed to the irresistible need that she felt her body caving to now. Maybe if she took over—took the lead away from him—she could have her man and enjoy it too.

Bracing her hand against his chest, Gigi gave a gentle push and broke the trail of kisses Roman had continued to use like a weapon against her restraint. She slid from the stool and he looked down at her, eyes cloudy with lust and confusion.

Gigi hooked her finger in the belt loop of his jeans. Using her hold like a leash, she pulled him towards her room. "Bedroom," she whispered, tempering that single word into a seductive promise.

As the back of his knees hit her raised mattress, Roman stewed over the change in Gigi that had swept over her during their breakfast conversation. She'd come out of this room looking wary of him and a little bit sad. Now, she'd turned back into the self-assured seductress that seemed more like a defensive front, rather than the real woman beneath. That changeable nature made him question whether he should be standing in her bedroom at all. At the same time, it was those very glimpses—brief as they were—that told him she would be worth it. That she was nothing like Jessica.

Those green eyes, they were his guiding light. Leading him past the façade she wanted others to see. For the public, she projected a sweet-tempered professional. In private, she allowed a select few to see her as a sexpot. Both those masks were a part of her, along with countless others he'd likely encounter along the way. Occasionally with him, she'd let them all slip away. In the kitchen, she'd been real. She'd been exposed. Undone by him simply calling her his girlfriend. He was falling for that woman.

Gigi gave him a small push that sent him crashing backwards into the mess of her unmade bed—the bed he'd tucked her into in the dark hours of the morning to sleep off her pain. The flick of his button popping open and the rasp of his zipper filled the silence. He reached down to still her hand. "Stop, beautiful." His voice was horse with his strained control.

She looked up at him through her thick lashes,

her green eyes filled with that vulnerability—his weakness—as she knelt on the floor in front of him. "Please, Roman. You've taken such good care of me. Why don't you want me to take care of you?"

What was it that held him back? Because she was right. Since they'd started this dance that first night in his shop, he hadn't allowed her to return any of the pleasure he'd given her. He'd held that piece of himself back while trying desperately to chip away the layers of her resistance—digging for the woman underneath. Now here they were, in her bedroom about to make love, and he was still limiting her access to him.

Roman released her hands, moving them to cup her face and caress the rising heat in her flushed cheeks with his callused thumbs. He had to pull the trigger—trust her or walk away.

chapter 11

igi stared, transfixed by the quiet war in Roman's eyes. They swirled with his inner turmoil, like whiskey in a highball. Someone hurt him—if she had to guess, it was someone who treated sex as cavalierly as she often did. Why hadn't she known that?

Alarm bells flared to life in her heart. Her conscience—a fickle bitch she'd forgotten still resided inside her—whispered that she should end this before she broke them both.

Then he caressed her cheeks, his rough skin contrasting the softness of his touch. "I'm all yours, beautiful."

Fuck—the things it did to her heart when Roman

called her that. For others she'd been princess, baby, or even dirty girl. No man before him had ever called her beautiful. She'd never needed to hear it, not until he'd said that one word. Now she craved it like a drug.

Roman saw her—saw past all the barriers she'd flung up around her heart. Would he still trust her so much if he knew what she'd done before him? He'd only seen a small glimpse. For the first time she wished Roman could have been the only one—wished she hadn't needed to fill that empty void inside herself with hollow physical experiences.

It may be selfish, but here she could pretend the past hadn't happened. She would lay herself truly bare in a way she'd never given anyone else—fear and control be damned. After all, he was doing the same for her.

Claiming her mouth in a deep kiss that was equal parts gentle and intense, he continued caressing her face before threading his fingers in her hair as she dragged his jeans and boxers down his legs. She took his hard length in her hand and stroked his hot flesh slowly. When he released her from their kiss, his eyes flashed with lust as she stared into them, pumping his cock. She licked her lips seductively. His breath caught. With her free hand, she toyed with the trail of hair that lead to her prize. His breath caught as her nails grazed the taut muscles of his stomach.

Fisting the sheets with one hand, he leaned back, creating more space for her as she knelt between his knees. She circled the head of his cock with her tongue. When he hissed with pleasure, she flicked the flat of her tongue against the V on the underside of the head, working the sensitive spot.

"Holy shit." Roman's hips bucked once and then held perfectly still, his muscles straining under her touch.

Gigi licked the underside of him root to tip, slow and sure. His answering groan and the way his grip tightened in her hair spurred her on.

This man had cared for her. Taken her to bed when she was pliant and weak. He could have done anything to her while she was that drunk. She probably would have agreed to it. But he hadn't taken advantage of her. No. He'd rewarded the trust she hadn't known she was giving him and left her safely dressed in her bed. He'd given her medicine and made her breakfast. He'd taken nothing from her—only given her what she needed. Now she'd take good care of him.

Gigi took the tip of him in her mouth and eased down, building inch by delicious inch. He was too large to take all of him down her throat but damn if she didn't want to at least try. He didn't push her for more, didn't force himself down. He let her take as much as she wanted. When she couldn't take another inch she curled her fingers around the base of him, pumping her mouth up and down. In answer, he fucked her mouth. Each stroke down came faster than the last. His hips twitched under her, as his restraint failed—and god that made her hot.

"Beautiful—" his voice broke on a groan as she sucked him as far down as she could take him. "Gigi, I won't last much longer if you keep doing this."

She looked up at him through her lashes and stroked down with her mouth again.

With a warning growl, he pulled her off him. He gripped her by the arms and tossed her on the bed beside him. Her whole body shuddered in delight and a giggle bubbled up from her lips.

"What's so funny?" He crawled up her body as he spoke, prowling like a jungle cat.

She started to answer but gasped instead when he pressed his naked body against her still clothed one, rocking against the ache in her covered pussy. She took a deep steadying breath and he stilled over her.

"I like it when you lose control a little. I like that it was because of me," Gigi said at last, her voice a husky whisper.

His answering grin—like the cat that got the cream or was about to—made her heart stutter. "I'd like to see you lose a little of that poise, sweetness." He rolled them and pulled her up so that she was in a sitting position across his lap. "I think it's time I found your pink. It's been suspiciously absent."

Roman's lips found her neck, first a soft kiss and then a nibble. She drew in a sharp breath and he soothed away the delicious sting with the stroke of his tongue. A surge of pleasure rocketed through her in response, making her squirm as her panties flooded with the evidence of just how hot he was making her. His deft fingers found the pull of her zipper at the back of her dress and dragged it down. The metallic rasp and her panting breath seemed to echo in her tiny apartment bedroom.

"I never thought much of pink." Kissing her bare collarbone, he slid the shoulder of her dress down, exposing the rosy pastel lace of her bra. "But since I've met you it's become my favorite color."

He nudged the other shoulder strap down and her dress slipped across her heated skin to pool at her waist. "Is this just for me?" He palmed her aching breast through the fabric.

Gigi nodded, her words catching in her throat. When she did finally push them out, they were little more than a breathy whisper. "Yes—I'm burning all the rest."

Lifting her breast from the cup, Roman bent his head. First, swirling his tongue around the beaded nipple and then drawing it between his lips. He nipped her and soothed her. The repeat of his actions from her neck and shoulder on her bared breast sent a warning pulse through her pussy. If he kept this tease up, she would come before he even touched her there.

"Roman—please." It wasn't the first time this week he'd played with her and drawn that breathy whine from her lips.

He growled his approval around her nipple before releasing it with a soft pop. "Be patient. You'll get what you need."

Instead of touching her where she wanted it most, he continued where he'd last touched. This time lifting her other breast free and teasing that nipple in the exact same agonizing way. It felt so goddamned good and so goddamned infuriating at the same time. Her pussy was weeping in frustration and pleasure.

He pulled back, freeing her breast. "Do you have any more pink for me to find?" His hand slid up her thigh as he asked, caressing the edge of her sopping wet lace panties.

He was so close to where she needed him. Just a little bit more. His hand stilled, waiting for her answer. God—what was the fucking question? Color, he'd asked about the pink again. "Yes!" she moaned at last.

Rewarding her outburst, he slid one finger past the flimsy fabric barrier, stroking and then entering her pussy. It pulsed around the invasion. His free hand danced along her spine until he popped the clasp on her bra, freeing her heavy breasts. He bent his head once more taking one nipple back into his mouth as he continued the slow drag of first one finger and then a second through her, stretching her sex as he pumped in and out.

"Roman—I need more." She hated to beg, but

everything he was doing to her was on another level. She'd do more than beg if he asked it of her, but now she needed so much more. "We've had a week of foreplay. I need you inside of me."

Just like that, he rolled, and she was on her back, his hard body leaning over her soft one. His lips hovered over hers and he whispered against them. "Don't rush, beautiful. We've got all day and I want to savor you this first time."

When he put it like that, could she deny this man anything? She'd never felt so special, so cherished as he was making her feel in this moment, with these words. She licked her dry lips and nodded. She couldn't even speak to answer him, but it was enough.

Roman worked his way down her body—sucking on her earlobe, ravishing her neck, and leaving a trail of kisses between her breasts that had her pulse raging like a storm. He worked her forgotten dress down her hips as he went and slid it down her legs along with her panties, until she was naked for him.

Kneeling between her spread thighs, he looked down at her as if he was memorizing every line of her body. His gaze was a physical thing, like a paintbrush. Adding strokes of color to highlight and create shadow. He looked at her with a lustful gaze that reminded her of the way he looked at art that he envied, only far more intimate.

"I want to mark you." Roman's admission came out a possessive growl.

Damn—that was hot. He was already marking her in indelible ways that she could never explain. Why not this way too? But right here, right now, she wanted him to mark her body with his love, make her want no man but him ever. It was a challenge she didn't even need to give voice to. As her gaze swept from that hungry look on his face, darkened with his five o'clock shadow, down to the hard length of his cock that she'd already had between her painted lips; he would ruin her for any other man.

He lowered himself over her. Spreading her thighs with kisses and the sweet burn of his unshaven cheek against her flesh, he worked his way to her core. He reached back and hooked her knees over his shoulders. Then she felt his hot breath against her. Her thighs shook with her building need, all this waiting. God—she wanted him so bad. She held her breath until the moment his tongue stroked her pussy top to bottom.

Gigi cried out in sweet relief.

Once he began, the tease was over. Whatever fragile strength had acted as his restraint snapped and he ate her like a starving man. He lapped circles around her clit as if he'd been hungry for her from the moment they met. Maybe he had. Lord knew she'd been craving him as long.

Her orgasm built like a gathering storm, sending tremors through her like thunder in the distance. Roman had sent this tempest raging through her. It pulsed inside her pussy and she bucked against him, an echo of what he'd done when she'd sucked him. He slid two fingers inside of her scissoring and then pumping in and out as he concentrated on her clit. Then he sucked on it and her orgasm broke free like lightning, burning through her body. Gigi screamed. Her control gone as she held onto his hair, pressing his face into her.

When she lay spent, her hands fell away and he climbed her body until he claimed her mouth in a kiss that sent another rumbling of thunder echoing through her veins. God—they'd only just started. The taste of her own pleasure on his lips was so naughty, it was just enough for that side of her; the Gigi who usually came out to play. Tonight, that version needed to stay locked away. This man, the man that had given her that pleasure deserved the real woman. He'd be the first to have her with no masks, no rules or boundaries.

Roman reached across the bed, rifling through the pockets of his discarded jeans until he came up with the condom. He held it up like a prize and smiled at her. That smile was so sexy. That smile was just for her. She sat up on her knees as he rolled the condom down his hard shaft. She didn't deserve this man, but she wanted him anyway.

She crawled across the bed to him as he settled against the headboard. He took her hand and lead her to his lap. She knelt over him and he ran the head of his cock against her primed entrance. He cradled her face with one hand, staring into her eyes. She met his golden gaze with her emerald one, willing her to show him the love that was already building in her. The emotion she didn't know how to give voice to, just yet.

Gigi leaned her forehead against his. "I've never wanted anything the way I want you." The words were a whisper, as if the admission had ripped from her soul.

She hadn't even known she was going to say it—didn't believe she could have. It was as close to a declaration of love as she had ever made. And she did love him. She didn't know how he'd worked that magic, but somehow, he had captured her in a way no one else ever could have.

He slid into her then, pulling her hips down until she was flush with his, and his hard length fully sheathed inside her. She cried out, eyes squeezed shut.

He ran his thumb over her eyebrow and placed a soft kiss on her lips before speaking. "Hey, open your eyes, beautiful. Look at me while we make love."

She didn't know if she could, not after admitting as much as she had. Not with him filling her like this. Gripping her hips, he moved her against him and she gasped, her eyes flying open against her will. So much of what transpired between them seemed to go against the grain. Her hands slid from his shoulders, gliding up his neck. She leaned her forehead against his and moved. Rocking her hips, she rode him. Her movements building to a rhythm that matched the rest of their lovemaking—slow torture. He'd already broken her with the strength of that first orgasm. Now she wanted to break together.

His hands moved over her body, caressing her curves, stoking the fire inside of her higher. "That's it—take want you want from me."

"I want it all," she whispered against his lips.

Then they were moving. Still buried inside of her, he rolled, bringing her down to her back. Now their rhythm changed. Not faster, not yet. Harder. He pulled nearly all the way out and she cried out at the loss—a loss that was filled immediately when he slammed back home.

"Is this what you want, Gigi? Do you want me to take you the way I love you—long and hard?"

Fuck—he loved her and all she could do was moan out an incoherent yes. Did he even know he said it, or was he becoming as drunk on the sex as she was? She didn't care. Not he didn't stop.

She wanted them to break together and with each thrust, each smack of his flesh against hers, it came closer to a reality. He slammed into her with his lips on her neck and then sucking her ear lobe, tugging on it with his teeth.

"Come for me, beautiful—I need you to fall with me." His whispered plea against her neck sent a shiver of pleasure rolling through her as his hand continued working her between their crashing bodies.

It was exactly what she needed. The spasms, the savage relief that came with them broke free, gripping him as he thrust home and held. His body shook over hers. He pulled his hand free, using it to brace his weight off her smaller frame as the shudders of his own release racked his body.

His arms shook with exhaustion, their foreheads pressed together, but for once her eyes were wide-open—taking in the emotion pouring off him. He moved as if to pull away and she wrapped her shaking legs around his waist, pulling him down. Refusing to let him go. It forced him lower, onto his forearms, crushing their sweat-slicked bodies together.

"Not yet." She needed to hold on just a little longer. Needed him to anchor her.

This—what they had just done—had shaken every previous experience to show them for the lie it all had been. This was real and she needed to savor it just like he'd said. This is what it meant to be more than skin deep.

chapter 12

oman shut the bathroom light off and padded back to her bedroom. Leaning against the doorframe, he watched Gigi. His gaze drifted down the perfect arch of her body as she raised her arms over her head in a languid stretch. It reminded him of a satisfied cat basking in the sun, or in her case, afterglow. He'd put that sated smile on her face.

She rolled over to face him. "When you stare at me like that, it's like you're drawing me in your head or drawing on me. I'm not sure which."

Crossing the room to her, he slid into bed and pulled her into his side "Don't tempt me, beautiful. Your body is the canvas of my dreams."

Gigi turned to look up at him, resting one hand over his heart. How was he supposed to play it cool when she looked at him like that? If the look of shock on her face when he'd called her his girlfriend was any indication, she wasn't ready to talk feelings. Letting the L-word slip during sex was enough of a fuck up for one day. Impending pleasure had a way of loosening a man's lips.

No—he had a plan to ease her into this nice and slow. He needed to get back on track.

She traced an invisible pattern across his chest as she watched him. "When you were growing up, did you ever take turns with your friends drawing on each other with a pen?"

"As a matter of fact, I did." Roman smiled at the memory. "But I actually started with my dad. He worked the night shift opposite my stepmom. He'd lay down on the sofa and ask me if I wanted to give him a tattoo. I'd get out all my pens and markers to draw on him while he took a nap right there."

Things had been hard after Roman lost his mother, but his father and Ann's mother had always worked hard to make sure they wanted for nothing, including quality time. When Roman turned sixteen and started running wild, his father had been the one to buy him *Inked Magazine*. It convinced him that his art skills really could pay the bills and give him some direction, other than booze. His old man had one mission—neither of his kids were ever working in a factory. Mission accomplished.

"My girlfriends and I used to doodle on each other during recess. I always had to hide it from my mother and father." Her words were wistful, but laced with an underlying sadness.

From the photos he'd glimpsed in her living room last night, he'd assumed her childhood had been a comfortable one; not necessarily a happy one. Her drinking over her father last night and her tone now hinted heavily at that. After all, comfort didn't always equal easy or happy. As much as he may be tempted to go there and find out more about what drove her to dive into that bottle, he wasn't ready to leave this blissful state of afterglow.

Gigi glanced up at him and resumed her explanation. "Anyway—it wasn't fancy art like I'm sure you managed on your Dad. Ours were just silly doodles of hearts and flowers. Sometimes the name of the boy we liked."

Roman nudged Gigi's shoulder, encouraging her to sit up. One delicate eyebrow arched up in an unspoken question as she complied.

"Hold that thought," he urged her as he leaned over the edge of the bed to swipe his jeans off the floor and dig in the pocket. Finding what he needed, he dropped the clothing on the floor and turned, holding up his marker. "Can I draw on you?"

"You seriously carry a marker in your pocket?"

"Doesn't everyone?"

She laughed at his answer and he knew she was in before she started shimmying down the bed to lay out flat for him.

"My body is all yours."

The innuendo dripping from her words had his cock stirring to life all over again. "Keep it up, Gigi, and we're gonna be doing something else."

She licked her lips; eyes locked on his growing erection and grinned. "Promises, promises."

Roman stared at her, mesmerized. How did she do that to him—take a sweet moment and turn it into a sexually charged need.

Gigi sat up on her elbows. "I thought you were going to give me a Roman Bishop original?" Her expression turned pouty. "Art now—play later."

He shook his head clear of the building fog of lust. "Yes, ma'am."

Running the plastic cap down over her curves, he considered the possibilities. She shivered, but otherwise kept still. She'd mentioned she would like something under her breasts. With his current state of arousal that wasn't a good place to start if he wanted to get through this. If it were permanent, where would he want to mark her? Somewhere she could feel comfortable showing if asked, but also hidden if she dressed up, would suit her best.

When his capped marker reached the curve of her hip, he stopped. The spot was slightly sexual, but not overtly so and fit all his other criteria. Besides, she'd be able to watch him work as he drew. He lifted her knees and draped her legs over his outstretched one. His other knee bent up as he settled into a comfortable position to work.

Roman popped the top off the ultra-fine magenta Sharpie. Yeah, he bought a pink permanent marker. When he'd needed one, the stupid color made him smile. It served as just another reminder of how deeply wrapped up in her he truly felt.

As the felt tip slid across her skin, he had to wonder if her feelings were as twisted up in him. There were moments when he thought so. Since they began, but especially today, the mask she seemed perpetually inclined to wear slipped. It gave him the glimpse he needed to keep moving towards her—to keep loving her. She opened to him readily enough when things got physical, not so much when conversation turned to feelings or where this relationship might lead. If she wasn't ready to hear him declare his feelings, he'd draw his heart on her skin and show her.

Gigi didn't speak as he worked, but he felt the weight of her gaze. When he recapped the pen and sat up straight, she sat up, leaning her weight back on her braced hands so that she could get a better look.

He'd drawn a heart symbolic of both of them, like a heart carved into a tree with the initials of two lovers. Instead of their names he'd used things symbolic of who they both were separately, making a more beautiful whole when joined together. On the left half, he'd drawn layered gears like the ones in the shop's skull logo. On her half, he'd drawn a lace pattern, intricate and sexy, the way he saw her. Along the heart's right edge, swags of jewels hung like crystal drops from a chandelier.

"It's beautiful, Roman." She circled the design, not quite touching the impromptu art with her manicured fingernail.

"Just promise me that if you get one for real, you let me do it." He rubbed the back of his neck with one hand and looked away from her. "I don't want anyone else laying a permanent mark on you. I want that privilege for myself."

"Let's do it right now. No one is at the shop." Gigi pulled away from Roman to sit up on her knees. "I want to keep this forever."

The marker art on her skin may have started as a playful way to tease one another and enjoy the afterglow of their physical connection, but if she was honest with herself, this was so much more. The thought that it would wash off her skin made her sick. No, she needed to make this last forever.

"If you like it so much, I can draw it on paper for

you to add to your art collection."

"No—not permanent enough."

She moved off the bed and headed for her dresser. She pulled a pair of panties and bra from the drawer, then bent to slide them up her legs. She was halfway through putting on a clean bra when she turned back to find Roman still sitting in the middle of her bed, watching her.

"Get dressed. I'm serious. I want this," she said as she finished with the front clasp. "Why aren't you moving?"

Roman slid across the bed and grabbed his jeans off the floor. "This isn't something you can take back, Gigi. You have to be sure. I don't want any regrets later."

How could she explain this to him? True, she had no tattoos. Before working at the shop, she would have told him that she wasn't that kind of girl. She learned quickly there was no type. The only requirement was that you had to love art. Those who truly knew her down to her core—and they were few in number— would tell you art was her passion. If there was one thing she appreciated, it was art and the emotions it invoked. This hand-drawn heart undeniably summoned something from her, a sentiment she needed to preserve. More than that, it was about commemorating the first man to ever break through her wall, to make her want to do more than play at arm's length and then run away.

What Roman didn't need to know was that any other man would have been kicked from her bed ten seconds after he'd finished unless she thought she might get a round two out of him. Even then, she still might have kicked him on principle. Roman had been the first man she'd ever—cuddled. He held her and she let him. She joked with him, shared a story with him, and did something playful. Whether she wanted to admit it or not, she'd fallen pussy first into a relationship.

Gigi turned to the full-length mirror on the wall, apprising the dark pink ink on her skin. A soft smile played on her lips. "I'd regret it more if I didn't get it."

She caught his reflection in the mirror, standing behind her seconds before he gripped her chin and turned her to face towards him, his amber eyes searched hers. Then, bending down to close the distance between them, he grazed her lips with his. The kiss was tender and reverent—a subtle reminder of the night she'd baited him to taste her.

"Okay."

"Okay?"

The corner of his mouth quirked up. "Let's go get you inked for real."

They dressed in companionable silence. Her in yoga pants, a pink tank and a soft sweater. Him in last night's clothes, minus the bow tie and suspenders.

Gigi grabbed her purse off the kitchen island and Roman retrieved her keys. She raised an eyebrow at him with her hand held out.

He dropped them into her palm. "What? How do you think you got home? I couldn't put you on the back of my bike."

"Believe me I'm grateful and sorry that you had to take care of me like that."

"Don't mention it." Roman wrapped his arm around her waist and pulled her in for a quick kiss. When he pulled back, a satisfied grin stretched across his handsome face. "I like taking care of you."

Her cheeks burned with embarrassment. "Let's go."

Keeping her head down, she walked out the door and out of Roman's embrace. He followed a few steps behind. So far, he wasn't pushing about last night and why she'd blown up their plans in favor of self-medicating with wine. Sure, he'd mentioned it, but he hadn't pushed—yet. How long could that possibly last? She climbed into her tiny car and the passenger door echoed in the small space beside her. By the time she finished backing out of her parking space, she'd made up her mind. It was better to bring this up on her terms and now was her best opportunity. Right now, she could control.

Gigi took a deep calming breath before jumping off the proverbial cliff. "So about last night…"

"You don't have to talk about it if you don't want to."

"No—you deserve an explanation. We had plans and I blew them off because of my family's melodrama." There was no easy way to say this so she dropped it like the bomb that it really was. "My dad cheats on my mom and he was at the gallery event last night with his whore."

Gigi glanced sideways at him before returning her eyes to the road. He was watching her as if she was about to jump out of the moving vehicle that she was driving.

"You say it like you've known about it." His tone was laced with concern and a smattering of confusion.

Gigi lifted her shoulders and dropped them back down. "It's not the first time I've caught him, but it is the first time I've seen him take one of his mistresses out in public. I never expected him to be so blatant. He probably thought it was safe that no one would be there that he knew. Only I was. He doesn't know I work for you."

She chanced another glance. This time, something she said had put a scowl on his face. "Are you ashamed of working for me?"

"No." The denial left her lips before she even had time to process it. When she took the position at his shop that would not have been her answer. Now if anyone other than her parents asked she wouldn't hesitate. "John Duval has a clear vision for what is appropriate for his daughter. No matter what I want—a gallery at a tattoo shop isn't it. I hide many things but this I'm not hiding from anyone. Omission is not hiding."

Silence hung thick between them and she let it. She focused on the streets that would be vacant until church let out in another hour. The wholesome stillness stood as a direct counter to the turbulence beating against her insides. Long minutes passed until she pulled into the parking space beside the Indian motorcycle he'd left overnight so that he could take care of her drunk ass. The thought had her cheeks flaming with shame again.

Gigi turned towards Roman. She refused to let this conversation sour an otherwise beautiful day with him. Add that to the list of today's surprises, but here she was, and so far, her only regrets had nothing to do with him.

"My family isn't like most families, Roman. My father cares more about his image than us. My mother and I are just accessories to him that need to be perfect."

"I don't fit the mold—the kind of man you bring home to Mom and Dad. You gonna hide me?" Bitterness dripped from his words.

This question was baggage that had nothing to do with her and everything to do with those who came before—or maybe just one. It would take a special kind of cold bitch to throw away his love. Trouble was, Gigi had been that kind of woman. No, she wasn't. She was something else—something just as bad. At least the men who came to her bed knew what they were getting from her and more importantly, what they weren't.

Gigi might hide from the judgment of others but she was at least honest.

She hoped that honesty showed as she turned in her seat fully to face him. "Never. You're too important to hide."

Holding her breath, Roman's amber eyes held her still, as if they somehow hypnotized her into this perfect stillness as she waited for fear to win. He reached up and traced her brow with the pad of his thumb, down the line of her cheek. He buried his fingers in the loose waves of her hair. His thumb continued to stroke her cheek.

"No hiding for either one of us—promise me." His words were a challenge.

Could she rise to meet it?

She didn't want to be the next woman to let him down. It was scary to consider bringing so much of herself into the light for one person. She'd sat in his lap, naked, handing her body over to him. That hadn't made her pause. This was different. He was asking her to be emotionally naked and not just for him but with him.

"I promise." The words tumbled from her lips, small, but honest. With him, they didn't burn as a certain other promise had.

He used his hand in her hair to pull her in, sealing her promise with a kiss that burned away any lingering doubt. They were in this together now. She was in deep. He was marking her soul in ways just as enduring as the ink he was going to be laying in her skin.

Roman pulled back from their kiss. "One taste of you and I forget where I am." A cocksure grin split his scruffy five o'clock shadow. "Get your fine ass in my shop because there is not enough room in this car for the things I want to do to you."

chapter 13

As soon as the door closed behind Gigi and the lock clicked home Roman had her pressed against the glass. The cold found her heated skin through the thin layers of her sweater and tank. Her heart didn't have time to race with anticipation as his lips possessed hers.

She could drown in this feeling—this intensity. No hookup, one nightstand, or friend with benefits had ever given her this kind of high. Would it change after today or would it always be like this? This question cooled the heat in her veins. As his lips moved across her jaw to that spot—the one behind her ear that made her toes curl—that voice of doubt whispered poison words. How long had it taken her parents to lose this feeling?

Gigi pushed down those doubts and pushed Roman away.

"What's wrong?" He braced his hands against the glass on either side of her head, boxing her in.

"Nothing." She smiled up at him, carefully masking the turmoil. "You keep this up and we'll get sweaty before you can make my art permanent."

"I'll draw it again."

"No." She shook her head, her teeth sinking into the flesh of her bottom lip before she continued. "This drawing is special. It wouldn't be the same."

Hadn't they already hashed this out at her place? Frankly, she'd had enough deep emotional talk for one day. She wanted action. She wanted her ink and when it was done, she wanted to take him in the office the way she'd been fantasizing about all week. She didn't want to spend another minute being an emotional mess.

Roman pushed off the glass and walked backwards away from her, a crooked grin on his handsome face. "If it matters that much to you, I'll go set up my station."

When he turned away, her shoulders sagged in relief. Gigi moved across the space to the front desk. After years of no strings hookups, her first relationship had her on overload. Needing just a few moments of mindless chatter, she pulled out her phone and leaned against the counter, checking her messages. She'd been unplugged since the event started last night. It was bound to be ugly.

No surprise—two missed calls from Dick Pic and more crude text messages with photos.

Dick Pic: Look at all you're missing tonight.
Text me if you come to your senses.

It accompanied yet another picture of his less than impressive manhood, his date's manicured hand wrapped around the base as if that was supposed to entice her. Did she know he was sending a picture like this to another woman? Probably not. The man was a disgusting pig and at this rate, maybe a little stalkerish.

To be safe, she saved the voicemail recordings and sext messages with the others he'd sent. It was time to consider getting a restraining order. She hated to shine a spotlight on her own behavior but if this continued, she wouldn't have any other choice. For once, she was glad she'd neglected to block Chad. If she had, she'd have no physical evidence and with his access to her through her father, blocking him might not have stopped him.

The big surprise was who hadn't messaged her— Ann. Gigi expected her to be livid. Either Ann was cutting her a break because she'd been so drunk last night or she was planning to ambush her tomorrow, maybe both. Gigi sighed and pushed the mess away. Either it would be okay or it wouldn't. Whatever the outcome, she was not giving Roman up. Ann wanted her to settle down. She got it. Now she'd have to deal with the fact that it was her brother that tamed Gigi.

"I'm ready for you." Roman's voice cut through her thoughts, sending a shiver of desire coursing through her like an electric current.

Gigi left her phone on the desk and joined him at his workstation. He'd reclined the retrofitted antique barber chair, most likely for his access and her comfort. Before she sat, she folded up the bottom hem of her tank top, baring her midriff, and folded down the waistband of her yoga pants to uncover the drawing that started as post-coital flirtation.

She slid into the seat and fussed with her clothing until she was satisfied with his access.

"Black and white or color?"

"Color and be liberal with the pink."

Roman chuckled. "I might have been disappointed if that wasn't your answer."

"Ask a silly question..."

"You'll get a silly answer," he finished. "You've seen me do this but now that you're on the other side it's different. The first thing I'm going to do is the outline. If you need me to stop at any time, let me know and I will. I work from the top down. When the lines are in, we'll take a break unless you need one sooner."

As Roman went through his spiel, he laid out little plastic caps that reminded her of tiny thimbles—probably because she was about to be a pincushion in the name of art. He filled each cap with black ink.

"Okay." She twisted her hands together in her lap.

What do you do with your hands while someone is dragging a needle through your skin?

Roman wrapped one large hand, now covered in black latex gloves, over her fidgeting hands. His other hand held the tattoo machine at the ready. "It's not too late to call this off."

Of course, he would give her the chance to bow out of this. Beneath that tattooed tough guy exterior beat the heart of a gentleman. They were like a mythical fucking unicorn and she had actually found one. Her. The girl who slept around because she couldn't trust a man not to hurt her.

He stared into her eyes. His eyes that reminded her of a low burning flame with their amber glow that seemed to see so much of her. The black frames of his reading glasses slid down his nose making his heated look that much sexier.

"It's going to hurt, Gigi. Sometimes beautiful things hurt." His voice was low and rumbled across her skin like a physical caress, soothing her with its quiet intensity.

"Are we still talking about the ink?" So much angst between them today. It was like living in an episode of *One Tree Hill* or maybe *Miami Ink* was a better comparison. Those reality shows on TLC were full of that crap.

One dark eyebrow arched up as he watched her over the top of his frames. He could see her mind wandering as she fought to process this new intimacy where he seemed to know the subtext of all her words. "I don't know. Are we?"

Silence hung between them. He just waited, drawing the silence out. Alone as they were, no one would step in and save her from breaking. She turned her face away, focusing on the cars passing by the shop window. The sinners, having absolved themselves from last night's debauchery, were leaving church now right alongside the righteous few who had no idea. Her phone pinged in the silence like a horn from god bringing down her walls.

Gigi looked back at Roman. He'd sat still as a statue, waiting on her. "I want to hurt where I can see it." There, it was out and damn him for making her say it.

She was ready for love. With him. She was ready to feel this even if it hurt her. She took a deep cleansing breath. "Do it. I'm ready." And she was talking about more than just the ink.

She expected him to chase her confession with the same tenacity he'd been displaying off and on all morning. His expression betrayed nothing. He wore the same stoic optimism—a half smile that was somehow serious and irreverent at one—that she thought of as his neutral setting. Instead, the machine in his hand buzzed to life. The mechanical hum filled the silence surrounding them. He released his grip on her hands and arranged them out of his way.

Gigi held her breath and closed her eyes as the needle touched her skin. Her eyes flew open and widened with the dull burn as the needle moved across her skin and she breathed with it. The first moments were agony. Then so gradually that she wasn't sure when it happened, the pain changed. It became something good, something that brought her clarity. It allowed her to drift on the white noise humming from the tattoo gun and see patterns she'd been missing.

Roman pushed her to open up. With each conversation, he held onto the chase until she broke and gave him a little more than she had before, but he wasn't running hot and cold. He was giving her space. Allowing her to process her feelings and accept them before moving in for another painstaking inch. Sneaky bastard. She already loved him more.

Leaving his mark on her skin was more satisfying

than Roman imagined it would be. Something about Gigi brought out that caveman need to possess her. For her part, Gigi sat perfectly still and detached. For the first few minutes, he could see the pain in her tight expression. Then the creases in her brow smoothed out and she smiled. Her green eyes were open and fixed across the room. He worried at first but she chatted readily enough when prompted, so he let her zone out.

Now he turned his machine off, sat it on his workbench, and turned to smooth cocoa butter into her angry skin. A soft smile played at the corners of her lips as she looked down at her ink.

"Do you want to get a better look at it in the mirror?"

Gigi's smile brightened as she slid out of the chair, standing on wobbly legs. She reached out and steadied herself with a hand on his shoulder. She giggled softly. "Sitting still for so long takes more out of you then you think."

After hours of touching her with a black latex barrier between them, he pulled the offending gloves off his hands and tossed them into the trash. "That was a quick one. I finished your art in under two hours. Most of the work I get takes four hours or more. Imagine sitting that long."

"I can actually. This wasn't as bad as I feared it would be." She released his shoulder and traipsed to the back of the shop and the mirror outside the office door.

Roman followed, feeling a little like a starving animal stalking its next meal—or in his case, his next hit of Gigi. Holding off sex with her for the week they'd been dating hadn't just been about her. It had been about insulating himself from the impending addiction to her. Pleasuring her while denying himself had been an attempt at building some kind of resistance—an inoculation—and a chance to make sure when he did have her, it wasn't going to be just a one-shot deal. One thing was certain, he was going to need her and often. He needed her already.

Leaning against the wall, Roman crossed his arms over his chest and watched her. She stood in front of his mirror ghosting her fingers around the heart that stood out vividly on her ivory skin. Her green eyes fixed on the reflection of her art. He moved toward her, unnoticed until he combed his fingers through the soft tendrils of her dark hair, sweeping it to the side and out of his way.

His lips grazed the column of her neck and his fingers closed over her shoulders, drawing her small frame back into his hard body. "It's good work, but it's not as beautiful as the canvas it's on."

She sighed and relaxed into him. "It's perfect."

Roman slid her sweater down her arms as he kissed a path from her neck to her shoulder. He let it drop to the floor. Both of his hands slid around her waist and up her ribs, cupping the underside of her breasts.

"I've been touching you for two hours, Gigi." To his own ears, his voice was a gruff bass made coarse by his desperation. "Two long hours where I had to focus on the machine in my hand and color in your skin when all I wanted to think about was all the ways I could have you."

She shivered against him, drawing a groan from his lips as her ass rubbed against his cock. The barrier of their clothes making it just the right side of painful. He walked her forward towards the glass until her body pressed against it.

"Roman..." Her voice was breathy, fogging the mirror.

"No one can see us back here, beautiful." Roman's hands moved down as he spoke, sliding under the lowered waistband of her yoga pants, forcing them down further. "You're like a drug. One hit this morning only whet my appetite. I need more."

Encouraged by the catch in her breath and the way she pressed herself back into his touch as his hand stilled over her lace-covered ass cheek, he knelt behind her. "Tell me I can have another taste. I need you to say it."

Her tongue darted out to wet her lips and with a trembling voice she whispered, "Please, Roman—anyway you want me."

The reflection of her green eyes blazed bright, as if lit with fairy lights as she watched him push her yoga pants down her toned legs, leaving her panties in place. She stepped out of the fabric pooled at her feet and spread her legs further apart. His hands stroked up her thighs. Her own hands pushed up her tank top and unhooked her bra. Both dropped to the floor, freeing her breasts. The pink tips of her beaded nipples kissed the mirror's surface as she kneaded her supple flesh. Her eyes stayed locked on his as she played with them.

His naughty girl. It set his blood on fire when she did something so bold. His cock throbbed painfully against the zipper of his jeans. But it wouldn't distract him from what he wanted.

Roman caressed her thighs with one hand. With the other, he hooked a finger under the edge of her panties and pulled them to the side. He licked the hot seam of her pussy. He lingered there, lavishing attention on her silky folds until her thighs trembled. Then he circled her clit. The gasp that escaped her lips told him she was close already.

He eased two fingers into her, fucking her slowly as he suckled at the center of her pleasure.

The walls of her pussy pulsed around his fingers as they pumped in and out of her. She ground her pussy into him and he groaned against her. Her own moan following his in answer. He pressed his tongue flat against her clit, circling the tiny bud with firm strokes as she whimpered and braced herself against the mirror.

"Oh god please—please come up here and fuck me." The strained plea was enough of a command for him.

Roman eased his fingers from her body and stood, keeping one hand at the small of her back to hold her pinned against the mirror. With his other hand, he pulled a condom from his pocket and eased down the zipper of his jeans. He ripped the package open with his teeth before pulling out the condom and rolling it down his hard length.

Burying his hand in the messy waves of her hair, he kissed the back of her neck. A sweet, tender kiss. A kiss that promised everything he felt for her. "Last night, with a gallery full of people, all I wanted was to take you against this mirror." He ran the head of his cock against her wet opening as he confessed his fantasy, whispering the words against her neck. "I could imagine it so clearly all night."

He watched as she squeezed her breast firmly in her hand, her fingers drawing out the nipple and rolling it. Reaching around, he covered her hand with his own.

"Please, I need you now," she begged. "If you're going to say shit like that and make me want you this bad, you can't make me wait."

He groaned into her neck. "You used profanity—this must make you crazy for your tongue to slip. Do you even know how sexy you are? Do you know what you do to me?" Roman gave up teasing and pushed himself inside of her, his thrust pressing her hard up against the mirror, making her gasp. "Is that better, beautiful?"

"Yes!" she cried out, slapping the flat of her hand against the glass. Her voice was a breathless murmur as she continued. "I want to drive you crazy, the way you make me. All day I watch you, aching for you."

He rocked in and out of her, his crazy matching hers, thrust for thrust. This was not the slow, casual pace they'd set this morning in her bed. This was frantic. This was intense. The rhythmic beat of his flesh smacking against hers filled the silent void left when his tattoo machine had been turned off.

"Touch yourself, Gigi. Let me see it."

She reached down, sliding her hand down her flat stomach to her slick mound while the other hand braced against the mirror he was driving her up against with each thrust. When her fingers found her clit, a full shiver wracked her body. Her breath caught in her throat as her fingers danced over the center of her pleasure.

"That's right. Come for me and I'll follow." His voice was a husky command.

He was so close—so damn close—watching her touch her own body had him on a knife's edge. He just needed her to go over so he could follow. He gritted his teeth, determined to hold out for as long as it took. For her—anything for her.

Then her hand stilled, pressing down and she

cried out. Her body shook, her sex pulsing around him, gripping him tight. He wrapped his arm around her waist, holding her to him as her legs went limp, succumbing to a well-fucked boneless lethargy. He let go of the stranglehold he'd had on his own urges. The pleasure rocketed through him, a torrent of every pent-up feeling, and caged desire, spilling from him with his seed.

Still half-dressed and buried inside her naked body, he lowered them both to the floor before they fell. She turned in his lap and wrapped her arms around his neck.

Her head dropped to his shoulder and she sighed. "I am so keeping you."

Roman laughed. He loved this woman. Really loved her in a way he hadn't allowed himself even with his ex. He'd only known Gigi a few short weeks and she'd managed to get inside of him with every secret smile. She made him willing to take a chance again with every new inch she opened up to him. She was worth this pursuit.

chapter 14

gigi traced a lazy pattern over the black line of the sparrow and key tattooed on the side of Roman's neck. Like the rest of his work, vibrant teal and red dominated the image. She knew intimately now that more than just his arms and neck bore vivid ink. While she collected art on her walls from the places and moments of her life, covering every square inch, he'd done the same with his body. He didn't need to tell her why he collected tattoos the way he had. She knew. It was deeply personal and an unexpected connection. This link, this similarity—expressed on her walls rather than her body—is that what allowed him to understand what she didn't say?

There were plenty of words drifting through her now that she swallowed down. Sitting here content in the afterglow had her questioning that silence. Was it too soon to tell him that she loved him? He'd said it this morning when they had sex, but not since. No response was required in that moment and everyone knew what you said in the throes of passion couldn't be trusted. But if she said it now she had to worry about what it would mean if he said it back or worse—if he didn't.

"You're thinking hard about something." The rumble of Roman's chest against her cheek as he spoke felt like the best kind of heaven.

She could answer with the truth and let the chips fall, but no—she wasn't ready to be hurt yet. Because he would. Not on purpose. He wouldn't be able to help himself. She just needed her first and probably only taste of something good to last a little longer. She would do this relationship thing for as long as it lasted because it felt good. He would be her one lapse in judgment and when it was over, she'd retreat to the way it had always been.

Roman brushed a curl off her cheek with a work-calloused finger and tilted her head back to meet his gaze. The question was in his eyes. He wanted to know what she was hiding.

She'd give him the safe answer, but just as true. "Just thinking I want to go back to my place so we can spend the rest of the afternoon doing this."

He raised an eyebrow. "Is that all? Took you a while to say it."

She took a deep breath and let it out slow. "I'm not feeling rushed just at this moment."

He smiled at that and his arms tightened around her. God, he had a great smile. Any woman with half a brain and a pulse would fall for it. She sure had.

"Why don't you get dressed and go home." He placed a gentle kiss on her lips. Just a brush of his lips, but it set her blood on a slow simmer. "I've got to clean up my station and then I'll ride over. Shouldn't be far behind."

Gigi slid off his lap to the floor and began gathering her discarded clothes. "I'll stop and get something for us for lunch." She dressed quickly and turned to find him pulling himself together. "Is there anything special you want? I'm thinking Chinese."

"Orange chicken sounds good but I'd be happy with whatever." He planted another random kiss on her lips—more of a smooch this time.

They were turning into a real couple. Once again, she marveled at her own peace with it. The fear that usually sat like a pit eating at her was suspiciously absent. Instead, her stomach fluttered with happy butterflies—traitor. She couldn't afford to get used to this.

He took her hand and kissed her fingers.

"Before you go, we have to get you bandaged up. You'll only have to keep it covered until you get home and can wash it properly. You've seen the care instructions."

She nodded and allowed him to lead her by the hand back to his station. She held her tank top up for him and he lowered her waistband over her hips once more. He made short work of applying the plastic wrap and tape and then covered it with her clothing once more.

"Alright, get out of here so I can get this cleaned up."

"Don't be long," she said in a sugar sweet tone that did not sound like her own voice. Crap—did that sound to needy? She may have allowed her pussy to lead her into a relationship but she didn't want to become that girl.

He must have noticed her own wide-eyed shock at the words coming out of her mouth because he kissed her again and then smiled that crooked cocky ass grin. "Don't worry, beautiful. I haven't had enough of you yet." Then he turned away to pick something up off his work bench and so quietly she almost assumed she was hearing things he said, "Not sure I ever will."

Gigi stood in place, blinking in shock. Her heart beat wildly in her chest. Maybe he did love her.

His voice broke through her stupor. "Go on or we'll end up in my office next time."

She shook her head and started for the door. "Who says I'm not looking forward to that?"

Sass—she left him with a mouthy reply, which was more like her than what Gigi had wanted to say— I love you. Roman's remembered words buzzed along her exposed skin, raising it in goose flesh. They made her confession in her bedroom this morning feel insufficient. Even now, with takeout sitting on the seat beside her, all she wanted to do was throw herself at him the minute he came in the door and profess the feelings bubbling up inside of her. His words were like waking up. She'd been living in a daze and feeding her loneliness with empty sex.

If he really felt just like her this addictive ride didn't have to end. Maybe she didn't have to wait for the other shoe to drop. With this new perspective, a list formed. There was so much more she needed to make right. Once she confessed her feelings to Roman—regardless of anything he said—her mother filled the top priority. Her mother needed to know this kind of love existed out there. She couldn't possibly know or she wouldn't have stayed with their father for this long.

Gigi would straighten her out and then talk to Ann. She was less scared of Ann's reaction to the broken promise if Roman really loved her. He said he'd never get enough of her. She hadn't wanted to give that promise. Ann had dragged it out of her. Given the chance Gigi would break it again. She could do this. She could have a real successful relationship if she could just tell him she loved him. If she could just trust. Damn it—she finally wanted this.

Trust. Maybe she should trust Roman enough to let him in on the Chad situation. The idea felt like a dark cloud in her rosy horizon. Ann was the only one who knew. Gigi didn't exactly have a lot of girlfriends to confide in. Maybe she should do that before the rest of her list. If their new relationship survived that, then the LOVE conversation and everything else would be okay. That sounded like the best plan: Chad, love, Ann and then her Mother.

Gigi turned into the tenant only parking behind her building. She parked beside an unfamiliar BMW. Either someone had company or there was a new tenant. Either way, something seemed familiar about that car. There was too much chatter in her mind to focus on placing it.

She grabbed the bag of takeout and then got out of her car. She'd made it two steps around the side of the building when she realized where she'd seen that car because its owner was leaning against the very door frame where Roman had kissed her and given her an orgasm in full view of the street.

Dick Pic—her own personal devil come to drag her back to purgatory—drove that car.

Newsflash—she wasn't going.

Chad leaned against the doorframe with his arms crossed over his polo shirt. Expensive sunglasses covered the glare she could feel but not see as he fixed on her approach with a scowl. It didn't scare her. That was the face of a petulant child in a man's body because he didn't get what he wanted and what he wanted was her. What scared her was the fact that he knew where she lived. Looks liked she'd be getting that restraining order after all.

Gigi squared her shoulders and made for the door. "I told you I didn't want to talk to you anymore. Go away."

Before she could push past, Chad reached out and gripped her arm, pulling her to a stop. "And I said I wanted you. Your daddy said I could have you."

"Fuck you. I do what I want." For the second time today, a curse snuck out. She practically spat the words at him as though they were venom. This slip in her control had to stop and so did the games Chad tried to draw her into.

He leaned in, his overpowering cologne making her want to hurl on his shoes. "You already have, princess. Now you're gonna do it again."

Today felt like a goddamned miracle as far as Roman was concerned. He'd gained more ground with her in a handful of hours then he'd done in the previous week. The best part was that it wasn't over. Now he meant to enjoy the groundwork of their relationship instead of pushing for more. She was waiting for him. Wanted him. It put fire in his step to get the cleanup done and break down his station so that he could get back to her. He just couldn't leave the evidence of their sexcapade at the mirror for the guys to see. As it was he was going to be hard as a rock every time he walked past it to his office just thinking about taking her there.

His station was an easy enough break down. He had it done in no time. After wiping down the mirror and taking out the trash, he headed for the front. As he passed the reception desk a buzz rumbled from the direction of her computer. Retracing his steps, he spotted her enormous pink phone face down on the desk. Large as it was, the stupid thing might as well be a tablet. The fact that it wasn't attached to her hand had him smiling. For her to have been so distracted that she forgot all about it told him just how well fucked she truly was.

Roman picked up the device to take it back to her and made it two steps towards the door when the technical monstrosity buzzed in his hand with a quiet ding. He looked down at the lit-up screen as the alert preview flashing on the lock screen.

> Dick Pic: Where are you princess? I'm on my way over.

Hard plastic dug into his fingers. The dull pain radiated up his wrist, warning him to relax before he crushed the phone in his hand. Who was this asshole? Gigi swore she wasn't seeing anyone but him. The cynical voice that took up residence in his psyche after Jessica offered one hell of an argument right now: anyone labeled something as crude as Dick Pic had to be a guy. He sure as shit wasn't platonic.

Roman's stomach twisted up with the sinking feeling taking root. He swore after Jessica there'd be no more playing games. Trust was all he'd asked Gigi for and she promised it—a promise that seemed to mean very little now. Maybe he'd handed his heart over too soon.

No—Gigi wasn't like his ex. The intimacy, hard won as it had been, was more real than anything he'd thought he had with Jessica. The fact that Gigi gave it so grudgingly showed its worth. He'd asked her to trust him and not hide. He'd have to do the same and give her the chance to explain. But knowing that and feeling that were not the same thing.

Roman's emotions dangled perilously close to the edge of reason—hanging on just enough for him to recognize the signs. His skin crawled with simmering anger that felt ready to burst from his fists as he fired up the bike. He'd have to get himself under control before he saw her or she'd never open up. Problem was he kept sticking on the last part of the message— I'm on my way over. This faceless asshole could be there now. The message had only been sent a few minutes before.

Attempting to imagine a scenario where this turned out anyway but bad made Roman's mind stutter and did nothing to throttle back his mood. It also made the few blocks to her place fly by.

Roman stopped the bike at the red light on the corner.

Her building stood across the street and sure enough, Gigi was at the entrance. The expression on her face was a familiar one. Impatience and irritation—at first glance that attitude might have renewed his trust in his girl. It should have. The voice of doubt whispered another explanation. A lover's quarrel. Maybe he called her out about Roman, inspiring her wrath. She crossed her arms in front of her breasts, hip cocked out as her toe tapped. Then he caught the sneer on the face of the Ken-doll looking jerk in a polo who seemed to be the focus of her wrath. The asshat from the day he met her—the one she claimed was nobody.

The right course would be to park the bike and break up whatever this was. Find out the truth first hand instead of being a voyeur. What he should do versus what he wanted to do—that was the trouble. Did he know what he wanted? To be anywhere but here. For none of this to be happening and for frat boy not to exist.

The preppy douche reached out, gripping Gigi's arm. She snapped something at him and Roman could see him answer. Then he shoved Roman's girl back against the doorframe. She gasped as the forgotten bag of takeout slipped from her fingers and hit the ground at her feet. The douche crowded into her space, kicking it out of the way, as he covered her mouth with his.

Roman's pulse thundered in his ears, drowning out the traffic around him as it screamed out the rage in his heart. It narrowed the focus of his world down to where her lips met someone else's. In that second, he knew how little he'd loved Jessica. This feeling—this icy stab in his chest that seemed to cause a part of him to wither and die as if it had been frost bitten—watching a kiss that was so deceptively innocent in comparison to a blow job in a back room affected him so much more. The wound Jessica inflicted had been nothing more than a paper cut in comparison.

A car behind him honked. The world rushed back in, the *woosh* of sound deafening in his altered state of pain. The light turned green. He was holding up traffic to watch Gigi tear out his heart. He revved the engine and tore off, leaving her to enjoy whatever the fuck that was.

For a few brilliant hours, Gigi made him believe. Thirty seconds recolored every word that came from her lips. Her reluctance that made Roman believe the world was rose colored, now read gray with lies. It made the emotional bullet wound in his gut burn that much deeper. A bullet wound and a frostbitten heart. Served him right for playing with love, the gun had a mean kickback.

Pink's an ugly fucking color anyway.

chapter 15

Shock quickly followed by disgust slammed through Gigi as Chad's cold tongue jabbed at her mouth. A car horn honked and an engine roared as the driver peeled out. Damn—there were witnesses to this humiliation. She pounded on Chad's chest with her balled up fists. His response was to press harder into her. Like she'd enjoy the stiff evidence of his shrimp dick. Even before she'd been so gloriously fucked by Roman—who should be coming along any moment—she'd been unimpressed by the hype Chad failed to deliver.

She braced her palms against Chad's shoulders. He moaned into her mouth. Gag—she was about ten seconds from puking in his nasty maw. In desperation, she let her hand fly. The strike stung her palm as it connected with his cheek. As many times as she slapped this jerk, you'd think he'd get a clue.

Finally, he pulled back, rubbing his palm across the red mark she left with a grin. "Damn baby, I can give it to you rough if that's how you like it."

"You don't get to call me baby, you little arrogant prick." Gigi spat at his feet and wiped her mouth with the back of her hand. "Don't ever touch me again."

"There's nothing little about me—or do you need a reminder." He groped his junk as if it was some kind of prize.

Gigi laughed—to hell with this wannabe frat boy. "What I need is you gone. You, on the other hand, need a reality check and a ruler. Then you need to get out of here before my boyfriend shows up and kicks your ass."

She left the food where it dropped and charged past Chad before he could grab her again. She'd order pizza. Slamming the outside door behind her, she raced up the stairs—praying to whoever was out there that Chad didn't follow.

The thirty seconds she wasted with her hands shaking so bad that she dropped her keys twice, flashed at her like the countdown in a stupid bomb squad action movie, as she struggled with the lock on her door. Precious time lost that left her more vulnerable and exposed than she'd ever been. There was a certain amount of danger inherent in being a single woman who liked casual sex. She hadn't been blind to her risks. It made her vibrate with fury that when she made the conscious choice to settle down, this could still happen to her.

When the lock finally turned, she flung herself through the door, and slammed it behind her—locking and dead bolting it. She backed away from it slowly, eyes fixed on the handle waiting for it to rattle, waiting for him to pound on the door and demand entry.

Gigi sank to the floor. She had no idea how many minutes passed before her racing heart and hard breathing calmed enough to think past the bile still lodged in the back of her throat. The memory of Chad's cold prodding tongue forcing his way into her mouth had her scrambling up, racing to the bathroom to clean out her mouth.

Items clattered into the sink as she swiped up the bottle of mouthwash. She chugged it like a junkie looking for a fix, swishing it to let the burn chase away the nastiness. Holding her hair back, she leaned forward to spit it out and watch the blue liquid swirl past the fallen items. She turned on the tap to rinse it away. If only her wannabe stalker could be disposed of so easily.

Where was Roman? The burn of the mouthwash helped but she needed another taste of his lips and tongue to erase the lingering memory of Chad's violation. Nothing else would cut it. How pathetic she'd become in such a short time.

With the worst of the frenzy worn down to a dull edge, she padded back into the living room in search of her phone. She scooped her purse up off the floor where she left it. When her hand hit the empty space in the pocket where it should have been, her breath caught. NO—this wasn't happening. She needed to call Roman. She needed him now—like air—because she was drowning in emotion. She'd never waded this far out before, never used a pole to catch just one man instead of a net to bring in many and now she was going under.

Gigi, dumped the contents of her bag on the sofa. Change bounced off the cushion, clattering to the floor. A lipstick tube rolled under the coffee table. The detritus of her life spread out before her—but no phone.

Panic weighed on her shoulders, a heavy blanket, smothering her forced calm. Closing her eyes, Gigi straightened, pinching the bridge of her nose as she measured her breathing carefully. Here was her addiction—her and every other twenty-something American woman—her phone. She always had it on her—always—until Roman. Until he had distracted her with a kiss and words that made her ever-churning brain stutter and pause to feel the present in a way she never knew she'd always been chasing until she found it. Now, standing here with his absence she needed a fix.

What time was it anyway? She glanced across the room. The red numbers set the frown in deeper. An hour had passed since she left Roman at the shop. How long did it take him to clean? A smile tugged at her lips as she pictured him on his knees scrubbing the mirror and then on his knees for something dirty. She felt calmer already.

The front desk. She left the phone on the desk before she sat in the chair.

A hysterical giggle bubbled up inside of her. Smutty thoughts gave her peace and apparently mental clarity. Well, one thought did at least. The giggle turned into laughter that brought the sting of tears. Gigi collapsed down onto her sofa. She was crazy as fuck. What kind of her person functioned like that? Apparently, she did, and Roman wanted her this way.

She just had to wait for him. He promised. For the first time, she was going to trust a man to be what he said he would be—honest.

Roman felt her standing behind him. The heat of her presence caressing his neck and shoulders before he heard the soft click of the office door closing raised the hair on his neck in gluttonous anticipation. Eighteen hours of knowledge—of heartbreak at Gigi's feet or more accurately her lips—hadn't been enough to cool his body's reaction to her. He guessed no amount of time would. Disappointment burned in the hollow place in his chest left where his heart should have been.

Scrubbing his hand across two days' worth of beard, he turned in his chair, leaning back, legs spread, his glasses gripped in one hand, arms crossed over his chest as if he could hide the hole there. What he hadn't expected was to see the torment reflected at him through her red-rimmed eyes.

He'd never seen her without makeup. Even when they'd slept together she'd been wearing the remnants of the previous evening's cosmetic mask. But here she stood, face utterly bare and more ethereal for its absence of color against the backdrop of her dark waves. The combination made her green eyes standout impossibly large, eyes in which he once believed he saw forever. He turned his face away from the lies they told for her.

"I waited for you all night." The softly spoken words croaked out of her as if her vocal cords were as raw as her freshly scrubbed skin. It rang with bitter disappointment as if he was the one who'd fucked up.

He turned his whole body away from her, facing the wall—anything but her. "You left your phone on the desk."

The silence hung there like a physical being standing between them. There was another person standing between them—another man's lips that had stolen what Roman had coveted for himself. She had to know he caught her. She had to.

"I figured that out when I couldn't call you. What does that have to do with anything?"

"Why don't you ask your boyfriend?"

"I am. Unless I'm missing something, I thought we established yesterday, that's you." Gigi's fingers brushed his shoulder, her grip light; as though she wasn't sure she was welcome. Her touch burned through the thin cotton of his t-shirt and like a masochist, he wanted more, but that with the uncertain tremor in her voice was too much.

Roman tossed his glasses on the desk before he could crush them and stood, forcing her hand to drop. "I don't have time for this game, Gigi. I've got a client due in any minute."

She braced a staying hand against his chest that he shook off, making her face close down in confusion. "Your client can wait. I need to know what happened."

"What happened is that I thought I knew where we stood, but after that scene in front of your building yesterday, it's clear the position wasn't vacant like you led me to believe."

Her jaw hung slack and he could see the puzzle pieces drop into place.

"What you saw was a jerk who won't take no for

an answer. You're the one I want. I've never let anyone else…"

Unable to stomach another lie, Roman pushed past her. "We've rushed into something we shouldn't have. Now, I'm done with this conversation. I'm going to work." Opening the office door, he stepped out in front of the mirror where anyone could hear their business—where he'd last tasted heaven. He closed his eyes against the image of her naked and pressed up against the glass just for him. He shook his head to clear the invading memory and opened his eyes.

"I thought you were different." The words were whispered. Her pained expression, the tears gathering like a storm in her eyes, reflected at him in the mirror. Her next words came out stronger—they were the ones meant to cut. "That's why I trusted you—only you. Whatever else you think of me, I am not my father's daughter. I will never be that low and if you think I could do that to you or anyone else—you aren't the man I thought you were."

Her back ramrod straight, eyes cold and hard— she became the eye of the storm. She marched past him this time. Fragile dignity covered her like a familiar armor. Without needing to pause, she scooped up her forgotten phone and purse on her way to the door, which slammed behind her with all the force of a hurricane wind.

chapter 16

g od bless Vodka. Men let Gigi down but the liquid burn of her cocktail never did—and neither did Tinder until now. Sprawled out in yoga pants and nursing her cocktail, she scrolled through the listings on her phone. Too tall, too plain, too hairy, too bald—ugh and she'd already done that one. The neckline of her oversized t-shirt hung off her shoulder. She tugged her blouse up as she scrolled. What had she been thinking to fuck that? None of them were right. None of them were Roman.

Damn it—she was going to be a sexless spinster if she couldn't move on. She needed more liquid courage and a reality check from Ann to get through her first breakup. Ann would know what Roman was thinking.

Her friend would have dirt on the last bitch that fucked Roman over so that Gigi could blame someone other than herself. That wasn't quite right either. Aw shit—She should have listened to her friend, kept her word. No—she owed Ann an apology and a drink. Well, the liquor cabinet was open. There was no time like the present.

Gigi closed her app and dialed her friend—the sister of her lover. Former. She shoved the thought down and hit send. It rang twice before Ann picked up. Gigi opened her mouth to speak and began sobbing into the phone instead.

"Oh my god—you're drunk dialing me, aren't you?" Ann's annoyed sigh came through so clearly that Gigi could imagine the matching eye roll. "What did my brother do? Hold that thought—you're in no state to tell me over the phone. I'm sure this is going to end up more like Pictionary. I'm on my way over."

The line went dead. Gigi stared down at her blackened screen as she hiccupped through her tears. Had that just happened? Ann was always brisk and efficient, but Gigi couldn't make sense of Ann placing the blame on Roman without hearing what happened. It was backwards from everything Gigi expected. She pictured the look on Ann's face when she'd come up to Gigi at the gallery to warn her about her father and discovered Roman's possessive hand at her waist. That look did not match the words that had rushed from Ann just moments before.

Had everyone lost their minds? Gigi reclined her head against the arm of the sofa, balancing her cocktail on her stomach. She focused on the transparent pink liquid. She had lost her mind over a pair of amber eyes, fingers that played her as if he owned her, and sex that made her feel. Roman had lost his over what he thought he witnessed. Those all followed a twisted sort of logic. Ann's reaction was the one that didn't match the evidence.

Gigi wouldn't have to wait long. Only a quarter of an hour had passed when Ann flung the apartment door open. It struck the wall, bouncing the art off kilter. Ann neatly sidestepped its path before it slammed shut. "Don't you lock this thing? What if I had been Chad?"

"That piece of trash," Gigi slurred as she sat up thumping down her martini glass hard enough that the contents left a pink splash against the white painted surface of the coffee table. She hung her head, burying her face in her hands as a fresh wave of tears took hold—pissing her off further. "How do I shut these feelings off?"

"I'm on my lunch break. You have an hour to cry on my shoulder."

Gigi eyed Ann's power suit. Double shit—Noon. Kinda early to be this far-gone.

The sofa shifted under Gigi as her friend sat beside her. Ann slid her arm around Gigi's shoulders. "You better start from the beginning. How long did it take you to sleep with my brother and what did Chad do to scare him off?"

Leave it to Ann to get straight to the point. Again, none of this matched Gigi's expectations.

"You aren't angry with me?" She peeked sideways through her fingers.

Ann shook her head, her face pinched with dismay while glaring sideways back at Gigi as if she'd said something stupid. "Why would I be?"

Gigi turned herself to face Ann. She swiped at the tears still rolling embarrassingly down her cheeks. Ann's expression softened, her eyebrows raised as she waited for Gigi's answer. All she saw from her friend was sincere concern and confusion. None of the judgment she'd assumed.

"I broke my promise. I didn't even last two weeks before I messed around with your brother." Gigi let the admission hang, blinking back tears.

"No, you didn't. I mean you did obviously sleep with my brother or you wouldn't be in this sorry state now, but you didn't break your promise."

Ann crossed the room to the desk. Opening the center drawer, she reached in and pulled out a pink leatherette address book. She flipped through the pages as she walked back to the sofa until she came to the section she'd been seeking. Her finger scanned down the page. Smiling she closed the slim book and tossed it onto Gigi's lap.

"Roman's name isn't in your book. He isn't a toy

for you. That's what you promised me." Ann smile faltered as she sat down and put her arm around Gigi as she hiccupped on new tears. "My brother's an idiot. I've been playing matchmaker from the start and now you love him, don't you? I told that ass to take care of you."

Mouth hanging open in a surprised O, Gigi stared at Ann, blinking slowly.

Her friend continued in her usual rambling style. "I don't even know what happened yet, but I know he didn't listen to me. You aren't the problem. I delivered him my best friend on a rose gold platter and he screwed it up."

In the way a child would stroke a worry blanket, Gigi thumbed through the pages of the small book in her lap. "It's not all his fault. I should have told him about Chad. I planned to, but not soon enough. Maybe then when Chad kissed me, Roman would have trusted me."

The last thing she should do was defend the man breaking her heart, the only man she'd ever given access. Of course, she hadn't really given it to him. He pulled it from her piece by piece, until there was nothing left to do but hand it to him. The least she could do was own up to her part in all this.

Ann leaned away from Gigi as she spoke. "What? Chad was at my front door. He kissed me and Roman must have been close enough to see it. He thought Chad was my boyfriend."

Ann dropped her head back in apparent exasperation. "I told him to watch out for you. That something was wrong. That ass—he never listens. Never did when we were kids either."

Gigi should have seen Ann's subtle manipulation sooner, might have seen it if she hadn't been so absorbed in her own issues—in Roman. In the end, Ann's role didn't matter. Roman asked for trust, then refused to give his. She'd opened herself up, shared pieces of herself—gave him the trust she'd been denied. If he'd shown her the same trust, he'd have given her the chance to explain. All along, he'd acted like he understood the way she was and why without her having to explain. He gave every indication that he understood more about her than she would ever say. He'd taken her sordid past in stride—until Chad. Roman and her first foray into love had let her down.

Gigi pushed her vodka cranberry across the coffee table. The pink cocktail sloshed over the edge of the glass, adding to the streak of slopped liquor. "Vodka drowns other people's stupidity. Have some. I've got some Ben & Jerry's too. If the booze doesn't cut it, the sugar high will."

Ann took the offered drink, slugged it back and then slammed the empty glass on the table in front of her. She coughed and shook her head. "I'll pass on that ice cream. The liquid fire is enough for the ass I'm about to kick."

"I've got this. You just hang in there." She patted Gigi on the knee. "My brother is going to come groveling. The fool just doesn't know it yet."

Roman picked at the label on his beer bottle. He alternated between peeling it off in long strips and twirling the bottle to find a fresh patch to ruin. A row of bottles stood like naked brown soldiers between him and Billy, who happened to be tending the bar tonight—the same bar he'd met her in—and the douche she cheated on him with.

He gave her credit for having the balls to admit she knew what he caught her doing, but they must have been made of solid brass for her to go on insisting she hadn't been cheating from the start or even just in that moment. It didn't matter how he felt about her— he would not be played for a fool.

Despite this conviction, branding her as another heartless bitch, ate at him as false. Images of Gigi, the anger she'd been projecting when the douche laid his lips over hers. That had been a real emotion, not her mask. Even after two short weeks, he felt he could see the difference. His broken heart tortured him with the confusion in her expression when he'd called her out on her bullshit, the shock and pain drawn all over the pretty lines of her face.

His heart was working on false data, he reminded it, as he tipped back the dregs of his beer.

Sunlight cut a line across Roman's hands, as the door to the bar opened and the fall of heavy boots echoed through the nearly empty bar. Declan slapped the bar top in front of Roman as he dropped into the stool beside him.

"I covered your 10 am and rescheduled the rest." Declan scowled at Roman when his announcement was met with a silent nod. "Don't bother thanking me or anything."

Roman hung his head between his elbows, braced wide against the padded edge of the bar top.

Billy swiped a towel over the space in front of Declan and sat a fresh bottle of beer in front of each of them. "'Bout damn time you got here to talk sense into our boy."

"Nah, this fucker was talking sense at the start." Roman clapped Declan on the shoulder. "He warned me not to fool with Gigi. Just had to get my dick wet though. From now on, I'm listening to him, Billy. Not your romantic clap."

Declan's nostrils flared as he leaned away. "You mean crap."

"No, I mean clap—like a goddamn disease. 'Cause that's what love is." He took another pull from his fresh bottle, but it soured in his stomach and did nothing for the lump building in his throat.

Billy grabbed one of the empty bottles and pointed it at Roman. "I'd lay good money you're wrong. You got a good girl there and you're gonna be eatin' those words before long."

Ignoring the old man, Roman glanced sideways at his friend. Declan's knuckles had gone white from his tightened grip on his own bottle. His tone was low, almost a threatening growl when he spoke. "I'm glad you're taking my advice now. 'Cause you're not going to like this but you *are* going to do it. I don't like admitting I was wrong about her but I'm doing it now. When you sober up—and I'll see to it you do—you're going to give that girl the apology she deserves."

"What the hell, man." Roman's jaw went slack as he did a double take at the vein pulsing in his friend's forehead. Damn—he was serious.

"She looked broken walking away from you. You got to watch her ass as she walked out. I got to see her from a different angle. From the angle full of tears and righteous fury. Jessica looked pleased with herself when you called her out and at times, she looked a little petulant about getting caught. She never looked that broken."

The front door crashed against the wall. "Ah, hell, you're gettin' it now," Billy groused, shaking his head.

Roman turned to see Ann stomp towards them in full business professional battle gear. Black designer pumps, white cigarette slacks and a tan blazer over a loose black shell, as if she was going to court or a hostile takeover instead of a relationship intervention. Only the best would do for his stepsister. She also didn't hold back, wasting no time smacking Roman across the back of the head.

"Stop—What's your problem?" Roman flailed his hands to brush her off while Billy chuckled. Declan's earlier emotional outburst shut down as he turned into the stoic façade he usually resorted to when Ann came around, which wasn't often.

"That's for being an ass to my best friend." Ann smacked him again. "That's for jumping to conclusions that broke her heart." Her hand lashed out for another strike. "And that's for making me come down here to fix this. I trusted you with her!"

Roman glared at her. "You're lucky you're my sister and not some dude or I'd lay your ass out for that." His chest tightened as he worked to contain his emotions, shoving them into the beer as he steadily drained it. Everyone seemed confused about who cheated.

Tossing a wad of bills on the counter, he tried to stand.

Declan shoved him back down onto the stool. "No runnin' away, man. You listen to her. Your sister and I don't agree on much but I'm with her on this. I know what I said in the beginning but I was wrong. Did you even ask Gigi about what you saw?"

"Ask her what?" Roman shot back. "That slime was kissing her. What's there to explain? She said I was the only one and I wasn't. I think you all are forgetting who wronged who here."

Crossing her arms over her chest, Ann huffed out her impatience. "You're an artist. There is always context to color an image. Think, moron. Did she look very happy about that kiss?"

"I didn't stick around to find out. She looked pissed before he did it. I was relieved until he shoved his mouth on her." Roman flung the words at them.

"You idiot." Billy spat. Roman had all but forgotten the man was standing there.

Declan turned Roman on the barstool and shook his drunk ass, making his stomach churn. "She was angry at him and you didn't jump off your bike and knock the shit out of him? If that had been Ann, I'd have turned his face inside out."

Blinking fast for a moment, Ann's eyes widened at Declan's slip before she shook it off and her face pinched up in concentration. "I tried to warn you about Chad. I should have listened to my gut and outright told you when she tried to laugh off his stalker ass. Roman, he's been harassing her for weeks. She went out with him once and he couldn't take no for an answer after that."

Roman stilled, his mind stuttering as he replayed the scene in front of her building through this new lens. Ann was right; perspective recolored everything.

If that was true… "I fucked up."

"Took you long enough. Now how you gonna make it right?" Billy barked.

"I'd start with groveling." Ann offered, but she was looking at Declan when she said it.

"I'm not good enough for that."

"Well, you better sober up and figure it out fast before she gets much more self-destructive." Ann warned as she started backing towards the door. "Based on the state of inebriation I found her in, you don't have long before she does something she'll hate herself for and I'm laying the blame square on you, Roman. My job is done here, so I'm going back to work."

Billy waved her off. "We'll take him from here, hon." Ann disappeared through the door and Billy continued with a pointed look at Declan, "Then you're next Declan. I'm taking a Weed Wacker to the thorns around your heart as soon as we're done with Roman's sorry ass."

Declan glared across the bar. "Just make the coffee and focus your meddling on him. We got enough problems right now, don't you think?"

chapter 17

fter spending some bonding time with her Keurig, Gigi was considerably more sober. But she wasn't taking chances with her Fiat—especially since her love life once again put her on the unemployment line. Roman wouldn't fire her of course, at least she didn't think so, but she couldn't imagine sitting at that desk while he touched other people's skin and not hers.

She mentally shook herself. Didn't matter. Uber existed for a reason. She could wallow in her pity party and return to the vodka cranberry. Instead she would take a wrecking ball to the things that brought her to this point—the backseat of a man's car. For once, it had nothing to do with getting off. Sure, the stud driving was eyeballing her like he wouldn't mind. Up until two weeks ago, the untattooed, Tinder-vixen version of her former self would have been intrigued. Instead, she viewed it as comical the way he divided his attention between checking her out in the rearview mirror, and making sure he didn't rear-end someone.

The newly tattooed, heartsick version of herself was ready to pass that torch on. She still wasn't convinced that the old version was wrong for having the no-strings fun while it lasted. Live and let live. It just wasn't for her any more—not when her heart wanted Roman.

Her mother was the top of her "To Do" list. Her father's poison had tainted Gigi's relationship outlook by association and ruined her mother. She needed her mother to see the light yesterday. If Leslie Duval saw it today, that would be a good enough start. The car pulled up in front of the stately white colonial that she'd grown up in. A sigh of relief snuck out when she spotted her mother's white Mercedes in the driveway and no sign of her father's Porsche. It was still reasonably early on Monday, but if he'd chosen to work from home, Gigi doubted she could have been brazen enough to carry this out. Her bravery only extended so far.

Gigi thanked the driver, and stepped out of the vehicle. Her first step up the flagstone walkway seemed to echo in her ears as if she were still wearing the kitten heels she'd had on the last time rather than her Toms.

Two weeks ago, she'd walked through this same door and had Chad's hand up her skirt turning her world sideways. Now she was about to totally upend it. She opened that door and walked through. The smell of her mother's pot roast wafting down the same hall where she'd stood and listened to her father sweet talk his other woman, right where her mother or anyone else could have heard. It was so blatant, as if he had no regard at all for his wife—which of course he didn't.

Gigi didn't even consider ratting him out. Her mother must know and must just be turning the other cheek. It had been easier to believe that. Gigi had never dared to ask; what if she didn't know? What if she did know and thought she was sparing her children and her reputation if no one else knew? What should have mattered was that a bad man was destroying a good woman—in the same way a bad woman destroyed a good man, to the point that he wouldn't question what he'd seen.

No more. Enough tears and bottled up pain had passed because of suffering in silence. Because of selfish people and their urges.

"Mom, are you home?" Gigi called as she pushed open the kitchen door.

Her mother stood in front of a steaming bowl with

a masher in her hand, pearls around her throat and an almost plastic expression on her face. It was like a twisted Leave It to Beaver scene. "I didn't expect to see you today, Gigi. What a pleasant surprise."

She'd lay money down that her mother wasn't going to feel that way in a moment. "Dad due home soon?"

Leslie nodded in understanding of the usual subtext—will Dad be interrupting us because I don't want him to hear this. "Oh no, we've got time. He said he'd be working late again."

Pulling up a stool at the edge of the granite counter that divided the kitchen in half, Gigi perched on the edge. "This is a lot of food if he isn't going to be home for dinner."

"I'll heat some up for him when he gets home. Not that he'll eat it. I'm taking a plate to the neighbor. He's a widower and he's not used to cooking for himself. His wife, Rebecca, and I were good friends before she passed." Leslie pushed the bowl across the counter near Gigi and sat on the stool beside her. "It keeps me busy to feed a friend occasionally, now that I don't have a house full of kids to chase around town."

Gigi hadn't considered her mother's potential boredom or lack of direction once she'd moved out. For the first time, she wondered if this June Cleaver act was her mother's own choice. "Why don't you do some volunteering? Is there something else you'd like to be doing?"

"I always assumed I'd go back to work when you all were grown. But your father said it would make him look bad. I wouldn't be qualified for much after so many years out of the work force." Leslie sounded like a wistful girl recounting an unrequited love instead of a lost career. "What good is a Fine Arts degree that hasn't been used in ages? I find I'm a lady of leisure for better or worse."

Gigi worried her bottom lip as she stewed on her mother's admission. Telling her mother what John Duval had been doing could hurt her in more ways than Gigi had considered. Her father neatly trapped her mother and isolated her from any kind of help other than her own children and maybe a neighbor. Perhaps this was why Leslie stayed with him for so long.

More pieces and layers to all the things that people do, the decisions they make. Did Gigi have any right to judge? Maybe not, but she could help her mother. Gigi would not leave her helpless the way John—she no longer wanted to think of him as her father—made Leslie assume she would be.

"There's something weighing on you, honey." Leslie's smile was that open smile, so encouraging and yet layered with sadness that the Botox and a bad marriage just couldn't hide. "You can tell me. Whatever it is we'll get through it."

Gigi took the opening, tentative, as if she was putting one toe in the water—or in this case, a few well-chosen words. "What did you and Dad do on Saturday evening? Anything special?"

Leslie's expression went slack and her tearless eyes dull with resignation. Her mother could already see the hit coming, but damn it all, she walked through it anyway.

Her answer came out monotone, lacking any emotion. "He was out of town on a business trip."

"No, Mom. He wasn't." There. She'd said it—the easy part at least.

Leslie drew herself up with stately dignity, transforming herself into a visage more akin to Jackie-O than June Cleaver. She exhaled two words. "Tell me."

"I have a job now at a gallery. We had an event on Saturday night. My boss sold Dad a painting and I saw him there with her. She wasn't much older than me and the way they hung on each other in front of all those people—it was clear they were together."

"Did anyone else see?" She stared straight ahead. No tears. Not yet. Her hands twisted the diamond bridal set on her left hand.

Gigi twisted her own ring, the promise ring John had given her mother. It had been on her right hand since her mother passed it down to her on her graduation. She mostly ignored its presence on her hand. "Chad was there from his office. My friend, Ann—you remember her, don't you? I'm not sure how many other people there he might have known. My advertising did its job and the gallery had a successful event." She'd leave out the part about getting drunk in the back to avoid an accidental run in.

The room was still, the silence stretching between them. Neither woman rushed to fill it.

Leslie slid the ring she'd been toying with off her finger and laid it on the counter. "I need a locksmith and I need to call your brother before your father gets to him. Your brother will know the best divorce lawyer. Your father hasn't won a case in years and the dissolution of our marriage won't be breaking his dry spell."

Tears threatened the corners of her already red eyes. If her mother wouldn't cry, Gigi still had enough in the well for both of their broken hearts. Leslie turned and pulled her into a hug. She sank into her mother's warmth. It had been so long since sincere affection had been in this house, this pristine stage of false morality.

"We're both going to be alright, Gigi." Leslie pushed Gigi back, swiping at her tears with the corner of her apron. It was a gesture that reminded Gigi of being young and scraping her knee. Only this time she'd scraped something far more important—her heart. "A man will not bring us down. We're stronger than that. We are going to be just fine. I promise."

She gave a halfhearted nod in agreement.

"No," Leslie commanded, still gripping her shoulders, "Say it. You must say it to make it a reality, otherwise it won't take hold deep enough. Let me hear you."

Gigi wet her dry lips and repeated her mother's affirmation. "We're both going to be all right. A man will not bring us down."

"That's my girl." Leslie smiled and it was open and real. Not plastic. "Now let's make those phone calls."

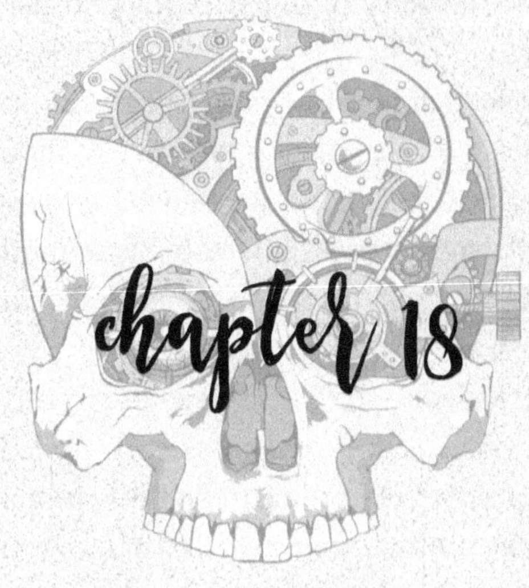

chapter 18

gigi stood next to the brick building that housed Ink Spinners with her bag balanced on the hood of her Fiat. Since she pulled into the parking lot, she cataloged the contents of her purse while sitting in her front seat at least twice, now she was doing it again. If anything was missing, even one item, she would go home. He probably wasn't even expecting her to come in. Which was even more reason that everything had to be right. Nothing out of place.

She'd spent two hours in the mirror painstakingly making over her messy hair into a dark waterfall of cascading curls arranged to fall over one side while the other side had been smoothed. Her makeup struck that delicate balance of temptress and business professional. As she chose her outfit that morning, a part of her wanted to drip so much pink it would make him sick to look at her. Not just a subtle reminder, but an all-out dig at the flirting she never should have done. Another side of her wanted to go severe with unrelieved black and white. That too was another kind of dig—a stark denial of everything that had passed between them.

In the end, she settled somewhere in the middle. Her high-waisted black pencil skirt buttoned up the front with a little left undone to give a hint of leg at the bottom. She paired that with a white formfitting blouse that gave a hint of the deep pink bra she'd been fully aware was too dark to wear underneath the thin top. The finishing touch that gave her the boost in confidence she needed had been the bright fuchsia heels, just couture enough to avoid being hooker heels.

Tomorrow she'd scale it back, or maybe next week. If she was going to brazen this out she wanted to make it painful for him, at least for today. Her mother had the right idea—no man would bring her down. Gigi wanted this job and if she had to look at Roman, then so be it. She didn't just need this job to pay her bills—she'd been good at it. She loved running the gallery space and elevating the shop's marketing potential. Being the boss's girl would have to be a benefit she learned to live without.

Gigi slicked on a final coat of Moxie Mauve lipstick, like war paint. She placed it carefully back in its designated side pocket, and took her first steps forward with her head held high.

"Shoulders back, girlfriend. Put some hip action into that strut." Gigi breathed in through her nose and on her exhale, she repeated her new mantra. "If mom can leave John Duval, high-powered attorney, I can do anything."

A low whistle sounded from across the shop. Roman looked up to see their new apprentice, Jasper, slack-jawed with his eyes fixed on the front window and then over in time to see Gigi through the glass seconds before she entered the shop in all her audacious glory. Hot damn—she had fire in her and she was here.

Declan, good friend that he was, took care of the kid by delivering a swift kick to the shin.

"Hey—what was that for!" The kid bent over grabbing his leg. But more importantly, he was no longer looking at Roman's girl, not that he had any right to call her that.

Declan turned his back to the room, directing

his words to the kid. "Respect, asshole." His gruff timbre carried anyway. "There's a lady in the room. I know it's difficult, but try to act like you're out of puberty."

Roman returned his focus to where it always should have been—Gigi. As she moved around the desk putting her things away to begin work, he couldn't help but let his eyes rove the lush curves that her black and white ensemble emphasized. Starting from the shocking heels, the shot of pink that made him painfully hard as he recalled the last time he let himself search for it, his fingers twitched to caress the silky curve of her calf.

His pencil moved over his sketchpad, allowing his imagination to trace what in reality he couldn't have. It might be the only way he got to touch her after all the accusations that she hadn't deserved. He didn't even merit this solace. Didn't matter—he couldn't help himself when she displayed her body like art, and that tease of color—he could almost see it taunting him through the thin material of her blouse as his pencil mirrored the rise of her perfect breasts. She knew exactly what she was doing. That's why she ran a gallery so well and ensnared his artist soul.

He had to have her back—had to make it right. And if she deigned to give him that elusive second chance, he'd spend the rest of his life groveling to make her Mrs. Bishop. To let her know that she was seen and that he could learn to listen instead of judge. The last thing she'd ever needed was his judgment.

The sharp squeak that came out with Gigi's indrawn breath broke Roman's flow. He blinked at the rush of his surroundings now that he'd fractured the tunnel focus she'd stirred. Her chair rolled back as she stood. "Dad. You shouldn't be here."

"No. You shouldn't." Her father's hand shot out as if to strike her, but she sidestepped him. Without John Duval's plastic blonde and the benefit of shadows he barely resembled the carefully put together lawyer he appeared to be at the event. Shit rarely did look good under the scrutiny of daylight.

"Get your things, you're coming home where you belong." He gripped her arm in one hand and scooped up her bag with the other, holding it out to her. "You are going to pay for that poison tongue and recant whatever vile lies you told your mother. I never should have let you think you had choices. You had your chance. Now I'm putting you in your proper place."

"This is my job. My place," she spat in a sharp whisper that carried nevertheless. "You're making a scene and I'm a grown woman. I'm not going anywhere with you."

Roman stood, moving without thought to loom behind Gigi. Declan was at his side without needing to ask. He was the kind of man Roman needed in a crisis.

Based on what little Gigi had shared when she'd attempted to explain her family, before Roman's assumptions had gone and fucked it all to hell—this was about to qualify as such.

Unable to resist the excuse to touch her, Roman removed her father's hand and left his own in its place. A gentle touch, one he meant to be reassuring. Her fingers ghosted over Roman's and then fell away.

"Is there a problem, sir? The lady just got here. We should allow her to settle into her day." Roman forced a smile that he was certain came off more like an evil grimace based on the pinched expression of Duval. "We would be happy to help you, wouldn't we, Declan?"

Declan nodded; his arms crossed in from of his chest, bulging his corded muscles so that they strained the rolled up sleeves of his white dress shirt.

Duval stood impossibly erect, as if he had a stick shoved so far up his ass he'd been walking on his tip toes. His neck was back, nose in the air, attempting to look down on them as he spoke, despite being the smaller man. "This is none of your concern. My daughter is no longer employed by this establishment lent."

"See, that's a problem for me. Last time I checked, I write the paychecks and she hasn't lost her voice." Roman took a step closer, crowding himself into the other man's personal space. "I'm not inclined to let you walk out of here with my Gallery Director and Marketing Manager. You see, sir, I need her. And I'm not about to allow you or anyone else to take that choice away from her." He hoped she could read between the lines of that statement because she went still under his touch, as if she couldn't bring herself to breathe.

The balding bastard turned six shades of red. "You can't be serious, calling this a gallery? No daughter of mine is going to waste a Bachelor in Art History and Business working for a dirty tattoo parlor. I don't think you know who you're messing with young man. I will have the health inspector so far up your ass—"

"Try it, old man." Roman stepped in until Duval walked backwards towards the door to avoid physical contact. Gigi's hands gripped Roman's arm, nails digging in through the white cotton shirtsleeve. "Leave my business now. And do *NOT* bother Gigi again. Next time I will not ask nicely and I'll have more friends."

Duval opened the door, putting it between his body and Roman's. "This is not over."

"Yes. It. Fucking. Is." Roman's fist lashed out, slamming on the doorframe beside Duval's head.

He squeaked out his cowardice as he fled, the door thudding closed in his wake. Gigi wilted, stumbling backward on her towering heels until her searching hands gripped the edge of the desk. She used it like a toddler trying to stand, working her way back to her seat to collapse.

Gigi leaned forward, scooping up the purse her father discarded on the floor. Her hands shaking, she carefully put her planner back in the bag, then her phone before retrieving her keys from the door where she'd stashed them. "Declan, I'm gonna need another day off. Can you walk me to my car? I don't think I should go out there on my own."

"Beautiful, are you even okay to walk right now?" Roman moved towards her.

"Don't call me that." Gigi's hand flew up like a stop sign, repelling Roman's advance.

She hadn't listened. Hadn't read between the lines or she hadn't processed it yet. He was hoping for the latter. Now, seeing in living color the example she'd been set for how a man treated a woman, it was no wonder she had so many walls up about having a relationship. Roman's actions yesterday, his false accusations were a fresh wound that proved her convictions dead-on. That's what he was up against.

"I'm so sorry." It wasn't enough, but he said it. Odds were her father never said those words to a woman, especially his wife and daughter. That made it more important for Roman to say it. He'd tattoo the words to his body if that's what it took.

"Why don't we call you an Uber? I can bring your car by when I close up tonight." Declan held his hand out for her phone.

She nodded, her eyes fixed on some point Roman couldn't see as she handed over the device from her purse.

Declan met Roman's questioning glare with a level one.

His friend continued in an even cadence. "Don't worry, Gigi. You're one of us now and we're gonna take care of you. No matter what you decide, you have a place here, okay?"

Her head bobbed once more. Gigi seemed to focus in on her own shaky breathing. Whatever was happening inside her must have been a tangled mess because she looked as if she was ready to come apart at the seams. The sass she'd come in with had snuffed out. He should hold her until it was all right again. Knowing he couldn't take care of her the way he had before burned like the hell that was no less then he deserved.

Declan, not Roman, held her elbow to steady her as she walked on wobbly legs to meet the car. They stopped at the door and she turned back. Her gaze held Roman. In that drawn out moment, he felt the pull to sweep her up, to carry her away from it all. And her eyes—it was wishful thinking—but their sparkle of unshed tears shone like Gatsby's green lantern on the end of the dock, guiding her former lover back to her.

Her teeth sank into her full bottom lip. When she

released it, her faint words turned out to be Roman's true beacon in the dark.

"You know where I am if you need me."

Then she slipped out the door, as if she'd never been there to give him the salvation he'd been searching for.

chapter 19

*g*igi fixated on those three little words. *I need her.* Had it meant what her heart wanted it to? Fuck—she hoped so because if not that parting invitation was only going to be more heartache for her. She leaned against the bar, twisting the ring on her right hand as she watched Billy finish pouring the seltzer into her absinthe.

This time the green fairy served a better purpose than making the pain go away—one healthier for her liver. It was a reminder. Roman could see deeper, attribute meaning to things that she never would have considered as he had with this sweet means of intoxication. Absinthe represented a strange kind of hope.

The deep rumble of the barkeep's gruff words pulled her from her thoughts. "You're lucky I still have this on hand, darlin'." He pushed the milky green spirit closer to her. "Ordered just the one bottle special."

"I guess I am lucky." She slipped her billfold from her purse. "What do I owe you, Billy?"

"Nothin' tonight. The liquor is yours anyhow. Roman already paid. It'll keep anytime you want it." He raised his hand, gesturing as though tipping an imaginary hat, and moved on down the bar to help the next soul waiting for their dose of firewater.

Since her workday had ended early, only a few regulars populated the quiet dive. Gigi sipped on her drink as *The Pretenders* played on the jukebox. She hadn't even had the chance to gauge Roman's reaction to her not-so-subtle attempt at wardrobe temptation before her father—no, she would not call him that anymore—before John had upended her day.

Something had changed with Roman. She couldn't put her finger on it since he'd been spouting crazy accusations. He protected her, said he needed her, and given her a ray of hope.

She would not be quick to forgive his easy dismissal of her honesty and faithfulness right out of the gate on their new love. With the appropriate level of groveling—preferably on his knees with that magic tongue—she would jump on the chance to have him back again. If he just admitted he was wrong and told her why, it would be enough.

More than Gigi had ever needed any random hookup, she had been jonesing for his touch. If this was what breakups were all about, she'd avoid that mess in the future. All she wanted was Roman—in her bed, in her life, in any way they could be together. They hadn't known each other long, but what she knew in just a couple of weeks of everyday interaction and marathon evening conversations was all she needed to know. Add in the way her skin felt like it was electrified everywhere he touched her, as if she was a lightbulb shining just for him, she was hooked. It would be Roman or it would be no one. *Please God, let that not be necessary*. She'd never make it as a nun.

Finishing her drink, Gigi scooped up her purse and wobbled as she descended from her perch on the barstool. Shit—either absinthe packed a bigger punch than she assumed or she shouldn't have worn those heels. Shoes—yep—let's blame that. Not the absinthe. It reminded Roman of her eyes. It was a silly, romantic, thoughtful gesture. Another of his skills. Something no one before him had ever taken the time for. Another reason he was the one. Hadn't she already been thinking that when she ordered it? Great, now her thoughts were on auto repeat.

She'd waited an hour. Time to walk home. It wasn't like Roman didn't know where she lived and where she drank. Maybe he wasn't coming after all.

Tears welled up and her lip quivered just thinking of it. Screw it all—now she was weepy. Yeah, she was way too close to toasted. That is some good booze.

She waved goodbye to Billy, who nodded back, then she pushed the door open and stepped out into the sun. She flung her arm up to shield against the assault on her eyes. Damn that light was bright after the darkness of the bar. The only thing for it was to head home and put herself to bed. Start this clusterfuck of a day over when it wasn't today. Contemplating the intelligence of mixing her emotional state, hundred proof liquor, and fuck me heels; she started down the block in what she hoped resembled a straight line.

Gigi had nearly made it to the building when a firm grip closed on her arm and spun her around. Her heart leapt up, ready to be happy. He did need her. He didn't let her down. For one brief second, she'd been almost whole. Then reality came crashing in, stomping on her heart where it lay on the sidewalk as she recognized the sick leer of the last person she wanted to see. For fuck's sake, this asshole didn't know when to quit.

"Listen, Chad, I'm really getting sick of telling you, leave me the alone. You've jacked up enough of my life." She jerked her arm—not caring that she'd probably have bruises tomorrow.

His grip tightened, his voice sharp with command. "No—you listen. You belong to me."

They'd skipped to a new scary level with that one command—one that left her bravado cowering in the churning pit of her stomach. The look in Chad's eyes reminded her of a feral creature, hard and at the same time wide with crazed fear. It fit him like pickles on PB and J—all kinds of wrong. As an otherwise successful lawyer who would be most women's pick for most eligible bachelor, he could have just about anyone else. That didn't stop him from bodily dragging her towards her building. It didn't faze any onlookers into helping her now. Instead, it gave them every reason to look the other way.

Swallowing back her rising bile, she managed enough voice to shriek, "Stop! I'm not property." She clawed at his fingers with her free hand as she pulled backwards against his dragging force.

Gigi lost one of her heels as Chad yanked her over the curb, nearly cranking her ankle in the process. His step never faltered. Her now awkward gait made her that much easier for him to control, until he had her up against a wall on her building. He stopped on the carpark side, not visible from the street. Everything about him was rigid and still. A kind of deadly calm that had been present almost from the beginning of his harassment, when he'd reached to grope her under her mother's dining room table.

Her breathing, on the other hand, came out in ragged pants. The blood pumping though her veins sobered her ass up in a hurry, as if she'd been doing shots of coffee instead of liquor. "Find someone who wants you. It doesn't have to be like this."

Chad gripped her chin with his free hand. He squeezed, forcing her mouth open and making it difficult to speak or cry out. "You're right. It doesn't have to be like this."

His mouth moved towards hers. She pressed her eyes closed—dreading the cold fish feeling of his lips on hers. Then nothing. They never touched her.

The slap crack of flesh hitting flesh broke the silence followed by a muffled shout that sounded vaguely like "What the fuck!"

Chad's hands fell away from her. Without him pressing her against the wall, she stumbled forward and into another set of hands—familiar ones. Only her tipsy hope had confused her before because this touch radiated warmth. The press of soft cotton against her skin as strong arms held her told her all she needed to know. She inhaled the aftershave she hadn't realized she'd been missing and then opened her eyes to look up into the enraged glare of Roman. There was pain in that look. Only this time it was for her, not because of her.

"I heard her tell you to stop before you crossed the fucking street and I was a block away, asshole. When a lady tells you no, you listen." The tick in Roman's clenched jaw matched the tight control in the low gravel of his tone.

Chad rubbed his hand along his jaw, testing it.

His once neatly combed hair now fell over one eye like a degenerate pirate; his jacket sleeve looked rumpled and pulled askew. "You don't know who the fuck you're messing with, man. You better mind your own business before I call the cops and have you arrested."

Roman opened his mouth to speak but Gigi beat him to the punch.

"Do it—I'd love to file for a restraining order." Her voice shook, and only the warmth of Roman's leather jacket combined with her cheek against his white t-shirt fed her enough strength to push through. "I've saved everything, Chad. I bet I can get you disbarred. I don't think charges of stalking and attempted rape will help you make partner at Daddy's firm. And if those videos hit the internet..." She let the ugly threat hang there.

The cold smile Roman directed at Chad was sexy—predatory pride. "You better listen to my girl. Damn hard to make that kind of shit go away."

Roman loved this woman and her sassy mouth. She shook like a leaf in his arms, yet she didn't hesitate to put her attacker—the douche bag she'd labeled Dick

Pic—back in his place. Hearing her threat, the moniker on her contact list made sense, along with her constant need to be on her phone.

When Roman first parked the bike outside of the Red Barron and looked up to see her abandoned shoe, a pink beacon in the middle of the sidewalk, he'd snatched it up and ran. Then he'd heard her ordering the douche to stop. She didn't beg. Not Roman's girl. That wasn't her style, even in a crisis. Seeing that piece of trash touch her, forcing her submission, snapped something inside Roman. That something snapped 48 hours too late, but he could do something about it now.

That punch relieved a coiled tension he had been carrying in his gut since Declan had altered Roman's perception of Sunday. Having Gigi pressed up against his side while she told off that asshole filled another kind of hole that his ex, Jessica, had left behind. Roman had a lot to make up for with Gigi, but now he knew that could happen. He never should have doubted his girl and he'd spend forever making it up to her if she'd let him.

Roman might be allowed to play hero now, but that didn't guarantee that everything would work out for them. Even her words at the shop could have been his heart hearing something that wasn't there.

To find out Roman needed to be rid of this ass-clown so they could talk it out. "Do you have a hearing problem? She said go."

Chad jumped as if Roman had punched him again, and he wished the little puke would do something just so he could justify lighting up his ass proper.

The pussy-ass lawyer pulled his haughty frat boy mask on, it appeared eerily like the one Gigi's father had flung at him this morning like a dagger. "You won't last. She'll get tired of you too and when she does I'll be here waiting."

"You hassle her again—whether she wants me or not—I will come for you." Roman paused as the smaller man moved forward either to pass or make a move. Idiot.

With Gigi clinging to Roman's side, he wasn't willing to risk her safety. Roman turned, giving Chad his unguarded left side. This put Gigi as far away from her attacker as Roman could get her without letting go—and there was no chance in hell he was doing that—but he needed to make this warning stick. Men like Chad didn't give up unless it was worth their while.

Reaching out he grabbed the smaller man's tie, pulling him in and up almost on his toes. Roman kept his voice low and menacing. "I promise you—I know people. I will make you hurt. Me and every resource I have will rain down on you like fire until you wish you had never said her name."

The MMA bad asses Roman sank his ink into at Hard Luck Fight Club would ride or die over something like this. They were a good bunch of guys and would think nothing of backing Roman up in defense of a lady. They were also scary enough to prove a point to a pencil-pushing douche without having to hurt him if it came to that. Roman didn't think of himself as sadistic, but the thought of watching Chad piss himself when they rolled up might be worth doing anyway.

Chad followed orders and left, giving them a wide berth as he tucked his tail and ran away. Although if Roman had to guess he'd say Gigi's threat held more weight in making Chad move along than Roman's had.

Gigi slumped in Roman's arms, exhaustion heavy in her voice. "I have not had enough coffee for this much drama. Take me upstairs, please."

Wrapping his arm around her waist, he pulled her firm against his hip before moving. She didn't object to the nearness. The tiny flame of hope burned a little brighter. He should temper it—he knew—she could be too exhausted or afraid to be alone. He might just be convenient.

Roman made short work of getting her up to her door and she had her keys ready. He half expected she would pull away and leave him standing in the hall. She didn't, but instead gently nudged him the direction she wanted him to go and didn't stop until they were in her kitchen.

Gigi leaned against the counter and he took the

hint, pulling back. At least he did until her hand shot out and gripped the front of his shirt. "Don't go." The words were soft, almost as if they were part of her breathing.

"I'm not going if you don't want me to, beautiful." Roman gently stroked her jawline where Chad had gripped, replacing that controlling touch with a better one, and directing her gaze up from the floor. "I just want to lock the door in case he's dumb enough to come back. Can I do that?"

Gigi nodded and released her hold on his white cotton shirt. Backing out of the tiny kitchen, Roman kept his eyes fixed on her, as if he might wake up and discover he'd passed out drunk again lamenting his mistake. He only glanced away to lock the door. Had the room been this small when he brought her home last time? All that colorful art on her walls crowded him until there was no room for air, let alone the feelings constricting his chest. He wanted to be here— wanted this chance to apologize. Rubbing the tightness over his heart, he took a deep breath and returned to his girl—at least he hoped she would be his again.

Turning back to face the writing on the wall and give voice to the emotions squeezing the air from his chest, he found her, still in the kitchen but with her back to him. She slid her cup out from under her Keurig. She turned, giving him a view of her profile. Tears slipped down her cheeks as she brought the steaming cup to her lips. Her shaking hands had the coffee slopping over the side of the mug, making her wince as the scalding liquid hit her fingers. She set it down again without drinking a drop.

Watching her—witnessing her careful control splintering gave him the motivation to speak.

"I meant what I said today. I need you, Gigi, and I'm sorry."

Gigi held her hand out to hold him off as she doubled over at the waist. A sob broke free. Pain lanced through his chest. He'd done that to her, put her through this. She straightened but leaned against the counter.

"Why." That one word came out raw, as if every ounce of stress filtered through it.

The ache in his chest told him to say the words that would take away both of their pain. "Because I love you. You're a mystery that I love to study every moment of the day—reading your moods and the unsaid words hiding in plain sight—so vivid I could paint them." He stepped into her, riding the spill of words until his chest pressed against her outstretched hand. "Your grace under pressure, and the fissures I see in that strength let me know you're real and honest—something I was too wrapped up in my own past to see."

Gigi turned her green eyes up at him; tears shimmered on the edges made them luminous. Her fingers dug into his shirt and she gripped, thumping the side of her fist against his chest. "You let me down. You changed me and then you let me down. You can't do that to me anymore."

"I can't promise you I will never hurt you—beautiful. All I can offer is that I will be a better man. Every day I will try to be a better man than I was before, I will never be those bastards that made you an object. You are not property to me, and I will never confuse your actions for hers ever again."

He pulled her into the circle of his embrace, leaving her arm smashed between them, still holding his shirt like it was a lifeline. She could take it off his back, tattoo it with her makeup—he didn't give a damn so long as she forgave him.

Gigi melted into his embrace but continued to stare up at Roman with shining eyes, waiting. He could see the question in her eyes before the words left her lips. "Tell me about her? Whose lipstick stains do I have to erase from your soul."

"More like claw marks. The day I caught my ex on her knees for somebody else was the day she should'a stopped mattering. I gave her too much power." It was only because of Gigi that he could see it. He meant it—every word. "But it's okay now. You tattooed your lipstick right over the top of those scars in your own unique shade of pink. Ink is forever."

He ran his hands up and down her sides, soothing her and sating his own starvation for contact. She sighed with content. "Roman, I'm sorry too. I should have told you about, Chad. I meant to tell you."

Leaning back, he tilted her chin up to look at him. "You're not taking any of this on your shoulders. Do you hear me? I asked you for honesty and then I didn't trust you enough to give you that chance. This one is all on me."

chapter 20

$g$igi's pain and guilt found a shocked mirror in the hard frown that creased Roman's face. Neither of them deserved to suffer another second of it. Not when they could erase it all and start again with a better understanding of each other.

"I give zero fucks whose fault it is. We're both letting it go." Gigi had never meant those words more than now. They were starting over. This second. There was no need to drag blame in it.

Roman shook his head and opened his mouth as if he might argue but she cut him off. "I want that afternoon back, with the Chinese food and just us, shut up in here, making love and figuring out what it is to be us. Not to get stuck in this thing that tarnished our start."

Lowering his lips to hers, he took her soft and sweet. A kiss that was more apology when she wanted passion. Conviction burned inside of her, fanning the flame of her rising desire for him—desire that had been building since that right hook downstairs and amplified by each soothing stroke of his hands. Patience had never been one of her virtues. She leaned into him, deepening that kiss, chasing his tenderness with her own raw need. She hooked her free hand into his waistband, her thumb toying with the button. He groaned against her lips and she opened to him.

Roman's hands moved over her body until both found her ass. He used his hold to lift her up, sitting her on the counter. She knocked over the forgotten mug. Hot coffee spilled across the counter.

He pulled back, resting his forehead against hers. The rumble of his rich laughter made her thighs tingle. He spread her knees and pushed the skirt up her thighs. His thumbs traced tiny circles moving further up the inside with each pass. "We're pretty damn good at making a mess, beautiful."

"Love's messy. Don't let it stop you. I'm not anymore." Her heart thundered in her chest. Those words—they were the closest she'd ever been to admitting her own feelings. Adrenaline spiked through her, like she was about to cliff dive instead of verbalizing her emotions. Giving her body to the one man who could break her—who nearly had—seemed easy in comparison. She'd never been this alive or turned on in her life.

Roman's laughter died as what she said seemed to register past his lust. "Are you trying to tell me something?" He slid those magic hands under her skirt and worked her tiny lace thong—black layered over pink satin—down her thighs. "I don't need the words. I know."

Slipping them over her calves, he worked the silky fabric past her one remaining shoe. Caught up in Roman, she had forgotten all about the awkward balance. She shifted to toe it off, but he held her ankle still and shook his head. He stepped back, letting her panties fall, forgotten on the floor. His golden eyes didn't leave hers as he reached into his jacket pocket for her matching hot pink shoe. As he stroked her calf, he slid the missing pump back where it belonged. "You have no idea the filthy images those heels inspire."

Gigi pushed Roman's jacket down his arms. He allowed it to drop to the floor with her panties. The color it revealed made her groan and her body flush with a new surge of heat.

It would be so easy to play along and talk dirty right back. It's what she would have done with any other man. Roman was uncharted territory and deserved more. There would be plenty of time for those kinds of words later. "I've never said it before."

"I know." He reached over his head and pulled his t-shirt off by the scruff of his neck, revealing still more color.

For a moment, all that temptation stole her words. She reached out, laying one manicured nail on his chest to trace the red-filigreed lock shaped like a heart. It lay over his sternum in a bed of roses, the matched piece to the swallow on his neck that flew carrying the key. He painted his past on his skin to speak for him. She would have to use actual words. "I want to."

He waited, not pushing or drawing it out of her as he had every other confession she'd made to him along their twisted path into this relationship. This had to be all her. "I have rules."

It was a strange place to start, but she needed him to know the full magnitude of this—how she didn't take this lightly. This was her making a commitment. The corner of his mouth quirked up as he slowly worked his way down the buttons of her blouse. His fingers tattooed an invisible trail one exposed inch at a time as he worked his sensual distraction. It somehow made the words easier to say.

"I don't sleep with people at work, I don't screw with people who matter to the few people I care about, and I don't do feelings." Roman counted each off with a kiss along her collarbone.

Gigi swallowed hard as his thumbs found her nipples through the lace of her bra—the abrasive pink material she'd worn just to tease him, scraping her sensitized peaks. Finding her voice despite the building pressure in her sex, she continued, "There are others, but those are the ones I let you break." She pulled his face up level with her own so that she could focus on the warm amber of his eyes. "I love you, so I let you. I fell so hard that you became the one thing I can't hide from."

Roman moved his hands from her breasts to frame her face, again mirroring her. "I loved you almost from the moment I met you."

Under the intense scrutiny of his gaze, Gigi smiled like the shy virgin she hadn't been since she was eighteen. Her bare ass squirmed on the wet stone counter. "I never believed that kind of fantasy happened. But you defy all my careful rules."

"We can make new rules together. And you can hide as much as you need. I'll always find you."

"Can we start with Kinky Wednesdays? I've gotten a certain fantasy stuck in my head involving you and my frilly apron." She waggled her eyebrows as she gave him her best suggestive smile.

Roman's shoulders shook with his laughter. Damn—she loved the rich sound of it. The reward of his joy gave her a new kind of pleasure that went beyond the carnal that she always sought out. She could become just as addicted to that feeling as she had the other.

"I'm almost afraid to ask, but why wait for Wednesday when I could do it for you now?"

"Right now, I want something else."

Gigi slid down off the counter, and shimmied out of her rucked-up skirt, then dropped her blouse and bra to the growing pile of discarded clothes. In nothing but the pink heels he found so sexy and the mark of his ink on her skin, she felt like a pinup goddess as she sauntered toward her bedroom. His hot gaze warmed her naked skin. For the first time, she felt like more than an object. She'd always believed there was power in that but no—this love that went under the surface held the real power.

Leaning against the doorframe to her bedroom, Gigi smiled back at Roman. He stood where she left him. A half-naked statue come to life and he loved her—just her. "You should order the takeout for delivery. It's early yet and you'll need to regain your strength."

His face lit up with what she hoped was wicked intent. "Beautiful, I plan to keep you too busy to do much more than answer the door, but I hear it's great the morning after."

epilogue

Sunday mornings in the shop were Gigi's favorite. This was especially true now that the oppressive heat of August hung in the air like a steaming wet towel. Air conditioning made everything better. It allowed her to enjoy the sunshine filtering in through the front window dappling her skin as she lay stretched out on the fully reclined barber chair.

Most of the time he came in to paint while she stretched out on the chaise in their corner to read a novel. Last month she'd caught on that he'd been painting her—just as she was—in her pink tank top and shorts, with a book in her hand. He'd rendered her as if she were a casual goddess. It hung in his place, above the bed. She almost felt bad about it because he spent nearly every night in hers.

Today it was her turn to serve as canvas instead of subject. The satisfying hum of Roman's tattoo gun mixed with today's soundtrack of Sara Bareilles and Adele. Roman let her decide the music when they came in to expand her new art collection. It allowed her to drift out on the slow burn of the needle carving a path through her skin.

"How you holdin' up, beautiful?" He looked over the top edge of his glasses, a sexy smirk halfcocked. She loved those glasses and often asked him to wear them to bed so he could give her just that look from between her thighs.

Gigi gave him a lazy smile. "You know…kind of blissed out right now. I'm glad we're getting this finished though."

Roman finally started working on the under bust tattoo she'd originally envisioned for herself. The lace like filigree, pink roses and chandelier swags of jewels, made her feel like a human piece of Faberge—her tattoo turned into so much more than she could have hoped. His illustrative style never failed to convey just the story she wanted told. They were taking their time, small sessions every now and again, so that she could savior the experience. For her she found the pain-pleasure paradox became a kind of meditation.

"Do you still think you only want ink where you can hide it? That really limits what I can give you." He rubbed coco butter into the inflamed skin, soothing the last of her newly laid ink.

"I like that it's our secret—something just for the two of us to enjoy."

Roman sat back, beginning his station breakdown as he spoke. "What if I wanted to put one someplace others could see it? Something we'd both have?"

He was going somewhere with this. The months with him taught her that he led her along with subtle suggestion. He may talk gruff and use crude direct language at times, but he meandered methodically in getting what he went after, especially with her. He'd never been underhanded about it, just gently persuasive while taking the long way around. Having the time to learn him like this, intimately, and letting him know her had brought its own unexpected rewards.

She pursed her lips, considering. "I never gave a couple tattoo any thought before."

"No names, I wouldn't want that—it's the kiss of death." He peeled his gloves off and got down on the floor. Down on one knee. He took her hand and began toying with her left ring finger. "What about here."

She blinked back tears. "Are you asking what I think you are?"

He reached down pulling something out of the pocket of his jeans. "Maybe, you could hide it with this." Covering her hand with his own, she felt the warm metal slid up her finger radiated his body heat.

"That way it's still our secret."

When he pulled his hands back, a pale green stone like a minty sea foam but bright and clear, rested on her finger. The grid of facets cut into the cushion shaped gem caught the light and shimmered along with its halo of diamonds. Even the subtle pink of the rose gold band resting on her finger struck her as lovely and elegant. An untraditional ring for an untraditional couple.

"Oh. My. God. Yes!" She slid off the chair and into his waiting arms.

Roman fell backwards onto his ass, chuckling between her kisses. "You didn't even let me ask."

"But I know the question." She claimed his mouth for another quick kiss. "You were taking too long."

"You'll really marry me? I wasn't sure you'd say yes."

Five months ago, she wouldn't have thought the answer would be yes either. How could she blame him for thinking the same? "You're the only man I could ever imagine taking that step with—the only one I can't do without. If that doesn't mean that I should marry you than nothing does."

Gigi nibbled on his neck, already working her hands up under his t-shirt so that her nails gently scraped along his ribs. He shivered at her touch and she moved her hand down to his waistband, circling forward until she grasped the button at his fly. That's where his hand closed over hers. She groaned her complaint and gave him her best puppy eyes.

He echoed her groan. "I know, beautiful. And we will, just not right now. We have dinner plans—see I had this whole thing worked out..."

"But wouldn't you rather have me?"

Roman gripped her chin and placed a soft kiss on her lips. "Always."

That one word—such a simple clean word—coming from his lips, it made her ache in dirty ways that he hadn't intended. *Always* held so much power especially now that should would have one.

His fingers trailed down her neck and breastbone, continuing down until he reached the leading edge of the ink he'd just finished. "If it depended just on me, you would already be draped across the desk in my office." He laid a tender kiss on her lips, an apology kiss—she knew the difference now that she'd been in a relationship for the first time. "Let's take care of your new tattoo. The sooner we go there, the sooner we can make it to your place to celebrate."

That promise made her move. She was out of his lap, handing him the plastic and tape herself. "Well then shake it. I have needs."

Roman had her covered and bustled out the door, straddling his bike in record speed. The grin on his face through the whole progression had one stretching her own normally serious expression to match the happy bubble she felt in her stomach. A wedding. She'd never even considered the possibility. But it was a happy one. If she wasn't in a hurry to haul Roman home to bed, she would have asked him to head across town so that she could share the news with her mother.

They spoke every day now that Leslie had started the court battle to leave John. Lots of laughter and healing had taken place now that both women felt free to simply be. Her mother owned denim—something casual—and had started her own small business. Leslie never did lose those skills from college that John had tried to atrophy out of her so that she could be his perfect show wife.

The other half of that equation, John, thus remained convinced of his own shitshow. Gigi's brother wasn't speaking to their father either. When Jack came home at their mother's request, he'd discovered the decline of the firm and started the process of transferring home so that he could take over with the full support of the other partners. Their father would not accede any of this without a fight. Gigi guessed they had only begun to see the aftershocks of her parents' separation.

Riding on the high of the moment, they made good time and Roman parked the bike in the lot behind her building. Anticipation coiled low in answer to the vibrations of his Indian motorcycle and her own emotional high. For a moment, she thought Roman changed his mind and couldn't wait to have her, but then he helped her down from her perch behind him.

He took her hand and led her away from the lure of her apartment and the privacy of her living room—they'd never make it past the sofa the way she felt right now if they'd gone up.

"What are you up to?" Gigi asked breathless as they jogged across the street.

He grinned back at her, amber eyes glowing with that flame that fanned her own fires, but kept his thoughts to himself. Aggravating but typical. He may wear his emotions openly, but expressing them was another matter. Instead of words, he showed her every day. Now, he could only be headed one place. The question had been an unnecessary one. The bar where they began on a chance encounter—a Tinder match gone wrong—waited at the end of the block.

They came to an abrupt stop and Roman pushed her back against the wall, just outside the entrance of Red Barron. His lips crashed down over hers and that rush—the crazy feeling like she was coming apart and yet resonating in perfect tune just like she did under his needle, only all pleasure rather than pain—it crashed into her like the first time. Every time echoed through her like that. Even the soft kisses made waves instead of ripples. Now she would have this always.

He pulled back, resting his forehead against hers. "I should have chased you out of this bar that first night and stole you away from that douche."

"I would have thought you were crazy. No—this is our story and I like it just fine. It's lead to beautiful art." She licked her lips and his eyes tracked the small movement with predatory lust. "If it makes you feel better, I did think about you that next day. I'd started to hope Chad would really stand me up."

Roman closed his eyes and sighed. "I'm taking you in their now, before I combust and drag you back to your place. I want you to know—I'm not taking any responsibility for this part." Before she had a chance to follow up on that statement, the door to the bar opened allowing laughter and the opening notes to a Journey power ballad to float out into the early evening.

Someone poked out his head and yelled back inside, "Their here!" It sounded like one of the guys from the shop, but she never had the chance to see before they ducked back in, taking the ambient sounds with them.

A burst of suppressed laughter bubbled out of Gigi. "Secret's out now." She pushed past Roman and jerked open the door herself. His hand at her waist, reminded her of his steady presence as she took it all in.

"She said YES!" Roman bellowed over the top of her head.

Everyone they knew erupted into cheers. They had quality not quantity but they showed up and they were loud. All the guys from the shop made it and the fighters from the gym that Roman hung out with, Declan who stood by giving sidelong looks to Ann who remained willfully oblivious, and of course Billy. Even her Mother stood front and center with a smile and tears that left lines on her face now that the Botox had stopped being necessary—not that it ever really was. Whoever was behind this—since Roman refused ownership—had thought of nearly everyone.

Ann broke from the group and enveloped Gigi in a hug that rocked her back into the solid wall of Roman behind her. "Let me see it!" She backed up and grabbed at Gigi's hand, leading her further into the bar. "Roman! You did so good! I knew you two would be so amazing. Can I be in the wedding? Can I help plan? I know you like to do events but I'm the matchmaker I feel like I should have a hand in this. So can I please?"

Gigi's face started to hurt from smiling so wide. Her precise and efficient friend, the devious schemer and career climbing badass had just come unglued like a kid. "Of course, you're going to be my maid of honor."

Roman's voice cut through the laughter and happy chaos as Declan came up clapping Roman on the back and shaking his hand. "We couldn't do this without my sister anyway. Or my best man." He looked at Declan with one eyebrow raised and a knowing grin. Apparently devious ran in the family even without a blood tie. "You down with that, Declan? I'm not taking no for an answer, dude."

"You caught me. How can I say no to that?" His

expressed matched his words, liked he'd just walked into a trap instead of his best friend's surprise engagement party.

Ann looked much the same. Her mouth open in a stunned little O of perfect nude lipstick, as if the implications of her initial excited request and weeks of matchmaking manipulation had caught up with her in an unexpected and unwelcome consequence and swallowed her whole.

Roman leaned down and whispered against Gigi's neck so that his words made her skin tingle as his breath stroked her skin like one of his paintbrushes on a Wednesday. "Enjoy the show, beautiful—wait—Mrs. Bishop. It has a nice ring to it."

Mrs. did have a lovely ring to it—and now so did Mr. Forever.

the end

DO YOU LIKE A GOOD GHOST STORY WITH YOUR ROMANCE? CHECK OUT THE HAUNTED ROMANCE SERIES BY CASSIE LEIGH!

Until Death Do Us Part

Available now from Broken Typewriter Press
The veil between life and death will part to bring two souls together...

MILLIE was a lonely spirit with no one but her house to keep her company. That changed the day the handsome new owner of her precious home moved in and said hello. She never thought she would have a chance to fall in love again. Now she is chipping away at her past and turning away from the light she thought she was waiting for. There is just one problem; the love of her afterlife is engaged.

Turn the page for a sneak peek.

Millie spied the real-estate agent through the rosette window of the attic. She loathed the balding relic that now lumbered up the sidewalk since the day he brought developers to tear down her home. Reason told her she should welcome that fool. He could be bringing potential company into her life. She turned away from the window where she sat perched day in and day out. It made her ache with sadness to see the proud farmhouse that she spent her youth in sit empty, no furniture or voices filling it up. But her feelings were not enough to make her welcome the agent.

Twin metallic clunks from outside broke through the stillness of the morning and sent a fluttering sensation running through Millie's midsection. She paced the dusty pine planks; the prospect of new life carried her nearer the door on each pass. She didn't need to look. It would be better if she kept her distance up here in the attic. Unexplained cold spots and footsteps that had no apparent source tended to scare people away.

When the jingle of keys and muffled voices echoed up the stairs, her curiosity won out. Surely she could get a glimpse of them from the stairs. There was no need to go down.

The front door closed with a thud that reverberated through Millie.

The droning voice of the real-estate agent assaulted her ears. "It's a fixer upper but the neighborhood is quiet and it's in one of the better school systems."

Millie rushed to the landing and leaned over the carved wooden banister. "Don't you mess this up," she shouted down at the agent, whose heavy footsteps she heard lurking in the front room. "Tell these people what a lovely home this was. I'm sick to the teeth of being alone."

Millie blew out a long breath, a habit that was no longer necessary. Why did she bother, the real-estate agent couldn't hear her. She rubbed her hands along the polished rail. It couldn't hurt to go down and take a peek at who the inept fool brought this time. Millie shifted back and forth on the balls of her feet, unable to hold still. No, they'll come to her. She just needed patience—a commodity she had precious little of, unlike time.

"The more we see, the better I like this house." A man's clear baritone echoed off the bare walls of the kitchen in tandem with the banging of cabinet doors. Millie supposed the man behind it was going through opening and closing them as he considered his purchase.

The potential buyer walked into the entryway, leading a woman by the hand towards the stairs where Millie sat. To the diminutive Millie, he seemed tall and dark. When he glanced up the stairs, sharp blue eyes met her own. Even from this distance, Millie felt captive to the vitality that filled them. Though she knew better, she felt as if there was something in that look just for her, some message she wasn't grasping.

He looked away, back at the woman he came with. The absence of his gaze broke whatever unlikely cord of communion had been strung between him and Millie. He couldn't have seen her, no one ever did. Millie's cheeks tingled, remarkably like blushing, if that had been possible. She raised a hand to her cold cheek. He certainly was the best-looking man that the portly agent had ever brought through her home and closer to Millie's age than most of them.

"Noah, I really don't want something that needs this much work," said the man's companion. "I just wanted to walk in after the wedding to our picture perfect starter home." The woman's blonde ponytail swayed as she shook her head.

The woman wore a modern, soft pink sweater that came down to mid-thigh of her form-fitting denim. Millie looked down at her own shapeless ivory dress. It hung past her white stocking-clad knees. Perhaps Millie could have had a better husband if she had been as attractive.

Noah started up the stairs, hand in hand with his future wife. They must have money, Millie assumed, because he appeared as richly dressed as the pretty blonde, with her collared shirt and pullover sweater. Her working-class husband and father would have called him a well-to-do lawyer's son, or maybe a banker. Definitely not the kind of man Millie was used to being around.

Mindful not to touch the couple as they passed her, Millie scooted out of the way. She made no effort to conceal herself further. The woman looked past Millie into the bathroom, appearing completely unaware of her presence. Noah looked right at Millie. She gasped and then ducked behind an open bedroom door, kneeling down. Her heart racing, she peered through the gap below the hinge. When Noah continued into the first bedroom without comment, Millie sighed in relief and moved back into the hall.

He must have been looking though her. It was silly on her part to continue deluding herself that he could actually see her. Just an over-active imagination brought on by decades of loneliness, she chided herself. Only children ever noticed her and usually only the very young. She took extra care not to frighten the little darlings.

"What do you think of this one for the master, Claire?" Noah asked.

"The closet is so small and the carpet has to go. It'll kill my allergies and my asthma will flare up," she whined in reply. Her cheeks sucked in and her mouth pursed in a pretty pout.

"I can fix that," Noah promised. He began to count off the benefits on strong hands that appeared rough and used to work, much to Millie's surprise. "Just think of the possibilities. This house is under budget and we were only looking for three bedrooms;

this house has four. The room adjoining this one could be turned into a master bath and walk in closet."

His plan sounded lovely to Millie. Someone to care for her home and remake it into a special place again, like it had been before her life had fallen apart.

"I don't want to live in a construction zone." Claire crossed her arms in front of her chest and took a step back. "I want move-in ready."

Millie's jaw dropped and she drifted up beside Claire. "Be reasonable, not every man offers to do something so monumental, you silly woman. Don't you see how lucky you are?" Millie asked, waving her hands in agitation.

"You'll have that." Noah reached out, resting his hand on Claire's arm. "We have three month's until the wedding. All I need is eight weeks."

"I'm listening." Claire looked away, as if only humoring him.

He moved in close, his voice lowered to a whisper. "I'll move in and start working. You stay in your place and focus on the wedding. You'll move in when we get back from Hawaii."

Mille held her breath, her hands tented together and covering her mouth as she drifted backwards into the hall. Was it too much to hope that this seemingly ungrateful woman would accept such a generous offer from her betrothed?

Claire sighed and her arms dropped to her sides. "Well, I'll get to pick my own finishes. I couldn't do that in a house that's already done, there's that at least."

Millie clapped in excitement and spun happily. Finally, some company.

Noah grinned and grabbed for Claire's hand. "I knew you'd see. Let's talk to Bob and put in our offer."

Millie beamed with hope from her spot in the hallway. Noah pulled Claire behind him, striding with purpose to the stairs. Millie stepped back out of the way until her waist pressed against the handrail. Noah returned Millie's smile with genuine warmth and a slight nod, silently offering a hello. He didn't pause as he continued down the stairs, leaving Millie disoriented. Her own smile slipped away. Did he see her after all?

ALSO AVAILABLE IN THE HAUNTED ROMANCE
SERIES

Follow You Anywhere

Available now from Broken Typewriter Press
*Looking in the past, two souls follow their intuition
to something more...*

BETTINA is letting go of the horrors of her past and starting over on her own terms. Used to the confines of her ex-husband's harsh restrictions, with her new friends at her side, she's excited to go on her first adventure in her unfamiliar small town life—a ghost hunt of an old Victorian boarding house. When strange events begin to emerge, Bettina is convinced something followed her home. He might not be the only one who followed.

Turn the page for a sneak peek.

By all rights, Seth should only have one thing on his mind: scare them off.

He didn't much like the look of the first two. The small one with the austere black hair was definitely a skeptic, and the colorful one looked tough. He had seen their kind before. They came with their scientific instruments, intent to prove to the world that every haunting was just misunderstood natural occurrences. It made them harder to convince to run, but it was a game he hadn't lost yet.

Through the years, it had taken him time to refine his scare tactics. The tools in his arsenal ranged from disembodied voices to moving objects. The only line he chose not to cross was violence, especially when those he chased off where of the female persuasion.

The key was to find a target who would make the others believe. The redhead who pranced around like a nervous spaniel would do nicely. Too bad he couldn't bring himself to use her like that. When he was alive, she was just the sort of girl next door he would have mooned over. Hell, he was doing it now.

There was something about her. Whatever it was, it halted his usual determination to wallow in misery. It might have been her timid approach to his front porch or the way she ran in through the front door because of its settling groan. Or it may have been that her auburn curls reminded him of autumn leaves and her amber eyes glowed like apple cider that once warmed his body in the same way that her skittish gaze warmed his soul. He may not welcome the intrusion, but dead didn't make him immune to her physical charms. It just left him without the means to make them lead anywhere useful.

He followed her as she moved around the table, gingerly perusing the instruments that her friends believed would reveal his presence.

"Tell me your name, beautiful."

"Amanda, I've got camera one and two set up where we talked about. Bettina, would you like to come with me while I take some base EMF readings?" The blue-haired girl poked her head around the doorframe from the kitchen.

Loud modern colors aside, the blue-haired friend reminded him of the women painted on the sides of the planes he had occasionally seen on base—harmless reminders of home meant to keep the boys happy.

His gaze followed hers, interested to see which one would respond and conveniently provide his answer. When the little one draped in black looked up from her screen, Seth grumbled his disappointment.

"Go with Charity and she can show you how we do things." From her answer, he assumed the one hiding behind the laptop must be Amanda.

"Um—sure, why not." His red head looked between her two friends before continuing. "What do you need me to do?"

Bettina. He turned the name over in his mind as

he watched her stroke the side of her flannel covered arms as if to ward off a chill. His gaze slid down her body, taking in the way her oversized flannel shirt grazed the tops of her thighs. The uniqueness of her name suited her equally distinctive beauty.

"Grab an IR camera and come on," Charity ordered.

Bettina looked down again at the table full of equipment and frowned.

Amanda reached over and picked up a device, shoving it at Bettina. "This one."

"Oh—thanks." She took the camera, a shy smile quirked up the corner of her full lips. "You guys are going to have to be more specific with me for a while."

Charity moved into the room and grabbed another device off the table, along with a flashlight. "You follow me with the camera on and I'll take the readings. We can start in the basement, and I'll explain things to you as I go."

Flipping open the tiny screen, Bettina nodded and together the women started towards the back of the house. Charity moved like a cat. Based on the saunter and sway of her hips she was secure in herself. In contrast, Bettina moved more like a timid mouse, trying to sneak away from the cat without notice.

Seth took a moment to enjoy the view Bettina offered before following. Black cotton leggings clung to the prettiest legs he had seen in years. Bettina wore them tucked into worn leather boots that came up to her knees and hugged just as tightly as the leggings. The fashion of this decade really was an improvement. It would be a shame to hide all that under the layers of a loose skirt.

If he still lived, she would be enticement enough to turn on the charm, something he never felt the need to do after the war and his recovery in Paris. No, he had been obsessed with something else.

Seth had been wallowing in his anger for so long that he had nearly forgotten what it felt like. Maybe, she could stay a little while. It was nice not to feel that burden of anger hanging on his every step, like the chains that Jacob Marley brandished in *A Christmas Carol*. He had built that chain link by link though the last years of his short life.

Their silent passage to the back of the house ended with the squeal of hinges that hadn't been oiled since he had successfully driven out the last owners of this house. Bettina shifted nervously behind her friend, device open and pointed over Charity's shoulder to peek into the darkness ahead.

Charity traipsed down the stairs as if dank old basements were nothing to worry over.

His girl approached the open door as if it was a gaping mouth intent to swallow her. She took a deep breath and threw herself into the inky oblivion. The rapid thud of her footfalls racing down the stairs echoed up at him.

Seth chuckled to himself as he followed. He

located her in the darkness through the glow of flashlights and her rapid panting. Someone should tell her that if she didn't stop hyperventilating she would faint.

Having found her, this was as far as he could bring himself to wait before he touched her. Just a light touch, stroking the back of her shaking hand. He could say she needed the comfort but he would only be lying to himself. A selfish need to feel contact, muted though it was, drove his actions.

A sharp indrawn breath punctuated Bettina's still rapid breathing.

Her friend swung the flashlight up at Bettina's face. "You gonna make it, Red?"

Bettina slowed her breathing by small increments, but he could see her shaking like those autumn leaves her hair resembled, clinging for purchase in the wind. "I'll be fine. Don't let me keep you from what you need to do."

No scream. Seth had expected more from a woman who seemed terrified by every step she took. But with cobwebs hanging from the floor joists above them, she may have discounted it as nothing.

Making her scream hadn't been the point of the contact anyway, and that should have sent him back up the stairs away from her. No good could come from this fascination with her. After all of that, there was only tingling in his fingers; he hadn't really felt her at all.

"You just need a distraction." Charity's voice was buoyant in the darkness. Clearly, she was in her element. "Have you ever watched one of those ghost hunting shows that talked about EMFs, EVPs--that kinda thing?"

Bettina shook her head in the darkness, sighed and then answered aloud, "Not really."

"That's okay, I can fill in the gaps. I just didn't want to tell you things you already had a handle on." Charity paused to scan a pipe with her meter and then continued on her circuit of the utilitarian space. "EMF stands for electromagnetic field and is man-made. So the point of what I'm doing is to establish what's normal for this house, before we stir anything up by asking questions."

"You've already stirred something up," Seth said, although he knew they couldn't hear. Sometimes he just needed the sound of his own voice to stave off his impending madness. It hovered over him in the endless tedium like a storm about to break.

Charity continued on her lecture. "Later if we observe a spike or a sudden drop we look for a reason. Sometimes it's a light switch got turned on, but other times—let's just say when we review the footage, we find something."

"Do you guys usually find changes?" Bettina's voice squeaked her question, like a mouse afraid to hear about the cat next door.

Charity shrugged, continuing to wander. "Not

everywhere we go and this is the first time we've been able to get in here. Probably the last time too. Still don't know how Amanda pulled that one off. Been trying to get in here forever it seems like."

Hanging on every word, Seth pulled it apart for anything useful. He may have wanted them gone before, but now the idea that this could be their only time here chilled his already icy veins. He was just getting used to the idea that he could like having someone here, especially Bettina. That she would leave—that just couldn't stand.

Seth reached for Bettina again, like a child stroking a favorite blanket for comfort. This time he stroked the blossom of her cheek, gliding his hand across her face and then lifting the curtain of her dark red hair to one side.

Her spine straightened and she glanced up, her eyes scanning the exposed joists above them. "Charity," she whispered. "Something is touching me."

playlist

The list of songs that shaped my words for Gigi and Roman evolved over the course of writing this book, but they were always on auto repeat until I finally typed out "the end". Enjoy the mood music.

Shape of You – Ed Shereen
Sing – Ed Sheeran
Say Is Right – Nelly Furtado
Don't Cha – The Pussycat Dolls
Make It Rain – Ed Sheeran
Sucker For Pain – Little Wayne, Wiz Khalifa, &
Imagine Dragons
Gangsta – Kehlani
Don't – Ed Sheeran
In Your Arms – Nico & Vinz
Guys My Age – Hey Violent
Sour Times – Covered by The Civil Wars
Gravity – Sara Bareilles
Whatever We Started – Richard Marx
Love Bites – Def Leppard
How Will I Know – Covered by Sam Smith
Everything – Alanis Morissette
I know – Fiona Apple
I'm Ready (MTV Unplugged Version) – Bryan Adams

CASSIE LEIGH writes contemporary and paranormal romance that's more than skin deep. Before she could write, she began dreaming up stories. Starting with recorded conversations for her dolls on a Fisher-Price cassette player, she moved on to an antique typewriter found at a garage sale, then an electric typewriter, and finally computers. It wasn't until she picked up romance novels in her late twenties that she found where she belonged. With the help of her husband, she carves out time to write while raising five children, working full time and obsessing over her laundry list of eccentric passions. Every new obsession seems to find its way into her romance world!

Want more? You can connect with Cassie Leigh online.

https://www.facebook.com/cassieleighauthor
https://www.twitter.com/cassieleigh322
https://www.amazon.com/author/leighcassie

To get the inside track on all new releases, sign up for her newsletter on her web site at

https://www.cassieleighauthor.com

BY CASSIE LEIGH

Haunted Romance Series

Until Death Do Us Part

Follow You Anywhere

Redeem My Broken Soul (coming soon)

Ushers Run Pack

Home For The Howliday

Bear Knuckle Baby (coming soon)

Ink & Brazen Women

Skin Deep

Leading Man (coming soon)

How About Never (coming soon)

www.ingramcontent.com/pod-product-compliance
Lightning Source LLC
Chambersburg PA
CBHW051843180726
48284CB00007BA/2023